Broken

3

Billie Dureya Shell

BROKEN 3

Front Cover Image By grafic designer Billie
Dureyea Shell & Kenny Writes

First Printing Edition 2021

ISBN 9781735023465

This Book Is Dedicated To

3 Of My 5 daughters
Diavion Shell, Shaniece Shell and Alura Shell
I love u all and know that everything I do is 2 make
life better 4 our family...
Daddy got your back 4life and even after

Love Dad

Family First

ACKNOWLEDGEMENT

⸺⊶⫸⊹⧉⊙⧉⧉⊷⊷⸺

First and foremost I would like to thank God without him none of this would be possible thank you for the many blessings you have bestowed on me I am eternally grateful and I will always put your face and everything that I do. To my mother Mclessie Shell I love you I'm so glad then I was able to put a smile on your face I'll get you the car that you wanted and I'm so glad you always keep me in your prayers because of you I know God was watching over me because of you I am the man that I am today thank you for teaching me what dedication and true commitment truly was I love you for always giving me 100% you taught me how to givw my family

100% I love you Mom. And now I understand all the things that you were trying to tell me. To my little Sister Glenda I love you and miss you and you no I always got you. To my beautiful Wife Shatoya thank you for loving me and always having my back

You are really my rib and you complete me I love you with all my heart and soul and I thank God for you everyday it's because of you that I believe that Angels really do walk with us because I met one and married her 1437. To all my kids I love each and everyone of you and every book I say your names so I don't have to do this time because your pictures on every last one of them Daddy love you y'all are the reason of my smile to my grandchildren Jordan and little Devon I love you guys Papa got y'all I just know in the future and in the present I'm making sure that you'll never want for nothing EVER......... Uncle Woody I love you you no that 2020 was a rough year for me I lost my people that I love but I know that you're in a better place in the name of Jesus I asked God to watch over you keep you all safe. Talk to God for me you all let God know even though I don't always make the best decisions I got a good heart save a spot 4 for me I miss y'all more then words can Express. To the big homie Rebo you will be miss VIP

To all my Dark Side Locstas 7s up YAAH...

Last but not least call my fans I love you thank you for having my back and believe in me I'm not going to let you down I'll keep putting these books out there..... y'all stay safe out there just covid-19 ain't no joke. But 2020 is over THIS 2021 FUCK COVID 19 AND THE MUTHA FUCCAS WHO INVENTED IT........

ENJOY THE BOOK
HAPPY NEW YEAR Y'ALL

Team Shell

PROLOGUE

—————⚜—————

Rashad I had to come up with a fucking plan to disappear quick! I had fucked up and I just did not know how I was going to tell Aniya. Man, what could I do? I thought to myself as I paced back and forth in the office of the strip club. We were doing good with our businesses and I just had to fuck everything up! She told me to quit and get out of the game, but I was being fucking hardheaded now the heat was coming down on me. I had got back in the game although I knew Mr. Richards was under investigation. Five years I started off small, no bodies, nothing! I wanted to be a kingpin but shit a nigga didn't want to get locked up behind the shit. My name wasn't ringing in the streets like I wanted it too and niggas thought I was soft. I was trying to be smart and not catch a body because the Feds would love to hang that shit over a nigga's head to testify. When Aniya seen that we were not making any dough after years of being in the game she told me to give the shit up. I agreed with her, but I just had that itch that needed to be scratched. I let this bitch Juanita make the runs for me. I was fucking her every now and then, but this bitch got caught up and snitched on me. They came for me HARD! They were quiet when they came and greeted me like a friend. They were on me every day and every night, letting me know that I was going to lose it all. When I asked them what they wanted they told me Al Richards. A nigga wasn't a snitch but what could I do. I made sure not to tell Aniya. Shit was moving fast in the investigation they had a nigga wearing a wire and everything. I felt like a hoe ass nigga every time I walked into a meeting with Mr. Richards. Two weeks ago, they finally locked up Mr. Richards and I felt a weight lift off my shoulder. Once that weight lifted a boulder came crushing down on my chest. They came to me and told me that I still needed to testify I was shook. This nigga Mr. Richards was going to kill me. He didn't know it was me who was going to testify yet, so I needed to get ghost quick. At first, I thought about telling Aniya, but I would have to explain everything. I was just not ready to do that. As I paced the floor and thought about everything my phone vibrated with a text. I looked and saw that it was Talia, my baby's mama. Talia 'I miss you.' I know I had told Aniya that her and my child were missing but I knew where they were. I would always know where Talia was at, she fucked with me through thick and thin. I had met Talia at the mall one Saturday while I was shopping. Talia was bad I mean Sanaa Lathan bad. She was gorgeous from her head to her toes. She gave me her number and told me that she was only in town with her boyfriend on some business. Yeah right you trying to throw that boyfriend shit in there I thought but you gave me the number. I wasn't even giving a fuck. She called me later that night saying her boyfriend was leaving her and she was going to be alone. I wasn't taking no chances though because shit hoes like to set up niggas especially out of town hoes. I told her to meet me at McDonalds, she did. I bought the bitch a meal and fucked her in the bathroom six weeks later she called me talking about she was pregnant. I was floored. She didn't know if it was mine or her man's baby. She kept it one hundred with the both of us and we waited for the nine months and took the test. It came back to be mine. Her nigga who they called the Reaper was pissed and kicked her out. She came to stay with me for a while but when she seen that I wasn't going to commit she up and left and moved to Jersey. BINGO! Talia, she was it! I needed to sweet talk Talia and go to Jersey with her and my son I missed the little nigga anyways. I went to see him every other month but this time I was going to stay. I loved Aniya and I felt like she was the one and I loved her kids, but I couldn't do this shit with the Feds. I looked over at the picture that sat on my desk of me and Aniya. I picked it up and stared at her beautiful face. Damn, what was I going to do? I had never loved anybody as much as I loved her. Yes, I fucked cheap ass hoes, but no one compared to my Aniya. Damn this was going to be hard, but I had to do it. I just had to come up with the perfect plan. My phone vibrated and snapped me out of my thoughts. I had to get my shit together. Between the Feds, my damn brother, Talia, Aniya and the kids, my Mama and Daddy, and my sister Rebecca I had to get things together. I looked at my phone it was Aniya I smiled until I pulled up the text. Wifey 'So you fucking, one of those stripper hoes again! I am gone fuck around and have to kill you nigga because you playing with my emotions.' What the fuck was she talking about, I thought to myself. I was about to text her that when another text message popped up. Wifey 'why get married if you gone fuck off? You could have just left my ass in Milwaukee with the dumb shit. You used to them dumb ass country hoes I ain't the one I am from the Ill Mill nigga' Oh, shit here she go with this crazy shit. She was always talking about killing a nigga and shit. Wait, wait. That was it I had the perfect plan. Yup Jersey here I come I had to get the fuck out of Atlanta start over get me a new life. I loved my wife, but she was just a pawn in this game too fuck it.

Chapter One
MYA

━━━◦◦≫≫⊰⊱◦⊰⊱≪≪◦◦━━━

I turned off the water and thought how great that shower felt. I had let my curly, long hair get wet while the water ran against my body. Being a mother of two children was harder than I thought. Thankfully I had my boyfriend Tre of the last five years because he was heaven sent just in the right time. The one night, Aniya and I went to a bar I had met him, and he had changed my life. His dark chocolate skin was not what I was used too, but I put my preference aside and got to know the chocolate stranger and it paid off. That night was a night to remember not only did I find the love my life, but we had also caught Niya's boyfriend at the time cheating. Hopefully he was at peace now because he was an evil man that had put my friend through hell. He was the devil reincarnated as Bruce Thompson. The man would stop at nothing to sabotage Niya, but from day one Tre had been heaven sent to me and Aniya. I thought about the time and knew I needed hurry to hurry up and get out the shower. I still had to check the books of the companies that Aniya had left in my possession and then I had to make sure I had the kids some food. Niya had left me in charge of her cleaning and home building companies. She had hired different managers. My job was to make sure the numbers looked good, that everyone was getting paid, and that all supplies was replenished at the end of the week. I did not do any of the firing and hiring but I did run background checks on the future employees and I always did pop ups. Being a spoiled brat who had nothing, but money handed to me I liked the idea of making my own money and being the boss. I could not have children, but I was a Godmother. Aniya had left me the sole guardian of her two children Malcolm and A'Deena. They were older so they pretty much could do things for themselves. Malcolm was a twelve-year old growing teenage boy and I loved that Tre had taught him certain things and always had time to spend with him. A'Deena was a ten-year old blossoming beauty that was sassy yet sweet. I adored those children but me taking care of them had been so sudden. Aniya had told me not to worry but I was worried, and I found myself stopping throughout the day to pray for my friend. Murder that was a serious crime, murder! I shook my head as I thought about it the whole thing was still unreal to me. How could my friend be on trial for murder? The last five years of Aniya's life was a complete blur to me because I had not been in Aniya's life in a while. It seemed like once Niya and Rashad got married Niya changed. She was always discreet and secretive, but she was really guarded and that scared me. Tre would always say you know she enjoying her marriage and her new family. Just think about what she has been through. Tre was always the type that looked on the brighter side and that is what I loved about him. Being a private investigator, he had seen many things but the things that we had found out about Niya's ex-boyfriend, was intolerable. I knew firsthand that Niya had been through a lot with her boyfriend Bruce. He was trying to sabotage her and take away the companies that her kid's father had left her. He was found dead in his apartment I knew Aniya was going through some kind of traumatic episode. She had married Bruce's half-brother, so something had to be going on in her head that no one was aware of. I wasn't the one to judge but damn to leave your ex-boyfriend and for his brother. I would never do that in a million years. I knew she had a thing for Rashad but to follow, through was too much. I had been supportive of her and the relationship, but it was strange to me. I tried to not think about the situation because it was too much. Matter of fact all this thinking was making my head hurt. I decided on some spaghetti and garlic bread for dinner something simple yet filling. Tre was going to be working a long shift because he was doing his job and he was also doing a side job for me. I wanted him to figure out what was going on with Niya. All my friend would say is that she is okay whenever she called which was seldom. How could she be when she was in jail facing murder charges, murder for killing her husband? This was something that I could not wrap around my head I just did not understand, and I really wanted answers. The day that Aniya had called to tell me to come get her kids it was a sunny afternoon. Tre and I had just come from a morning breakfast date. The pancakes with strawberries that we had with the whip cream had filled the spot and the sunny side eggs with the crispy bacon had me feeling sleepy. I just wanted to crawl in bed with my love and lay in his arms after that good breakfast. I had fallen in love with Tre and it felt so good. He was working so hard that he had not been around lately, but I was used to it. Plus no matter what he always came home to me. We had gone to the movies and for once our plan was to lie in the bed and just enjoy each other company at the end of the night. On the way from the movie theater my heart dropping call came in. I picked up and it was a jail call. You have a collect call from "Niya". That was all I heard, and I started panicking. I hurriedly started to accept but I did not have collect calls on my phone. I went through the prompts to put some funds on my phone. I dug through my purse and got my credit card while Tre drove and looked at me. He knew something was wrong and he wanted me to tell him. "What's wrong baby?" He asked. I had a one-track mind and was trying to register what was going on. Finally, as I punched in my credit card number, I answered him. "It's Niya she is in jail." He did not say anything because he knew that I did not know what was going on. My light face had turned to a red color and I my heart was racing as if I was the one who was locked away. After they had the money I was connected to my best friend. "Hello Niya?" It had been five years since I had taken over Niya's companies and Niya had gotten married to her husband Rashad. "Go get A'Deena and Malcolm. You know I put you as the guardian and I need you to call this number so you can go pick them up." She gave me the number. I grabbed a stick of red lipstick out of my oversized purse. I wrote the number against my light arms. I did not have a pen or paper and I did not have time to look. "What happened?" I wanted to know what was going on. "I killed Rashad." She said and my breath was taken away. Tre watched as my face lost all color. "You okay honey?" He questioned. "Wait, what?" "You heard me I am not about to repeat that shit." You could hear the annoyance in Niya's voice. "I told you if something ever happened to me to make sure you can get my kids can you do that until I get out?" She said and I shook my head yes although the only person who could see me was Tre. When I shook my head yes Tre took that as I was saying that I was okay, so he calmed down a bit. "Yes, I will get them. Do you have bail or anything?" I asked I needed to know what I needed to do and Niya was not making it easy because she wasn't telling me anything. "No just go get my kids." Niya hung up. I did not know what was going on but that was two weeks ago. Tre did not have any answers. He was using all his contacts as a private investigator but was coming up very short there was no jail records of Niya being in the jails and they had not heard anything. This was difficult and Tre said that he was going to get to the bottom of things. He was working overtime trying to get information, but none was out there. I believed in my man because he usually did so I was just patiently waiting because I was hoping that my best friend was okay. The fifteen second phone calls saying that she was okay was not enough and I needed to know more. It was strange because she was not calling from a collect number anymore so how was she calling? Tre had tried to trace the calls back to a phone line, but they were all throw away phones. If she had throwaway phones, then where was she at? All these unanswered questions that I needed to know because I wanted to tell her kids something. That was another strange thing the kids had not really said anything about what was going on. When I would ask them, they would just say my Mama is coming back to get us that is all she told us. As I slipped on my clothes I had so many questions whirling through my head. I just needed to occupy my mind by cooking. As I stood in the kitchen stirring the noodles the question just kept coming to mind. If she knows that she is coming back to get them what is really going on?

Chapter Two
MYA

—◦◦❯❯❱◦❮❰◦◦—

Niya and I had met in Middle School. I was always a quiet girl and so was Niya. Niya was always a pretty girl and I could never understand why she really did not talk to anyone. Niya always had short hair that was always kept up in a cute style. I on the other hand always had that curly long hair that I was proud to have. I did not talk to the kids in the school because they liked to keep up drama and gossip. My father had told me that the last thing a girl should be caught up in is some bullshit. All kids our age liked to do was talk bad about each other and to be honest none of them were anything special. All the girls dressed the same and wore their hair the same. All the boys wore the same clothes and tried to keep up with the latest shoes nothing was unique about any of them. I did not understand why they talked about each other. The day that Niya and I became friends was the worst day of my young teenage life. I came to school to find out this guy that I had a crush on made up a rumor about me giving him head. I had never put my lips on or near a boy's private area and for him to lie about that was really embarrassing to me. I had been quiet and had not said anything to anyone. I noticed the stares, but I just kept quiet. His girlfriend on the other hand was ready to fight her name was Sharita. Sharita did not like the idea of some other chick trying to get with her man. She had never seen me talking to her boyfriend, but she just went along with the rumor. Sure, I had flirted with the guy, but I never made a move on him. Sharita was a big booty brown skinned beauty that loved drama. Niya had heard all the talk about how Sharita and her three friends Raquel, Starla, and Nicole were going to jump me. It was lunch time and the girls surrounded me and started cursing me out. "Bitch your little prissy ass going to get your ass beat today." Sharita said with her stinky ass breath. "I don't want to fight you." I said in a calm tone I was scared because I did want to get jump and they mess up my pretty face. "Bitch you not going to fight me I am going to beat your ass." Sharita shot back and the crowd started laughing. "Whatever," I said and tried to walk away and that is when Sharita pushed me. She wasn't prepared for the lock that met her face. I had put a lock in a sock courtesy of my Mother who told me even if I got jumped to give them hell. I started swinging my hands and I clocked Sharita upside her head. It stunned her but Raquel came back on me and hit me in my head, and it dazed me. That gave the other girls the fuel to jump in the fight. They really didn't know how to fight, and I was giving as good as I was getting. Sharita screamed "Bitch want to fuck my man!" That is when Niya jumped into help me. She could not believe these girls were fighting me over a boy. Niya started punching the girls and since they were not aware that anyone was going to help me, they were not prepared for the blows. We all got suspended that day and Niya and I became best friends. I was beaten up a bit and had bruises on my face, but I was okay it could have been worse had Niya not jumped in. After that we were inseparable. Niya had met my father who was white and my mother who was black. I had met her mother and she was beautiful. I did not know if she was mixed like me because whenever I asked Niya where her father was, she would say gone. If I kept pushing the question, she would get upset. I told my

Mama about it and she broke it down to me. She told me that Niya probably did not know where her father was and that I needed to stop asking her, so I did. Niya would let me come spend the night with her when her mother would leave her on the weekends. I would sometimes ask Niya where was her mother. Niya would make up an excuse and say that her mother worked third shift. Although we were best friends Niya never told me anything about what she was going through. I was the one who talked. I talked to Niya about all my problems and she gave good advice but when ever I asked Niya if she had any problems then she would just act as if everything was okay. I had been trying to figure out how I was going to ever get in touch with Niya when I checked the mail and all my questions were answered. There was a letter addressed to me but there was not a return address. I was skeptical of looking at the letter for that very reason. It was late and Tre had not come home yet. I had put the kids in their room. It was better that the kids were older because they pretty much took care of themselves because I had never taken care of babies although I loved children. I cleaned up the kitchen and tried to watch television until Tre got home. My mind was restless and after a while I could no longer take it and I opened the letter and was surprised to see that it was from Niya. Dear Mya, Hey boo I know you worried about me but trust and believe that I am good. I hope my kids are being good I miss them so much. I remember the first time I found out I was pregnant by Hakeem it was the happiest day of my life which turned into my worst nightmare. No lie I loved the man to death, but he was an evil man. I know I am not the talkative type and I am not open. I have to let you know you are my best friend and every time I need you, you are always there. You are special to me because you never question me. You just do it and you are so sincere. Anyways I just wanted you to know that I am doing good and I am okay. I know Tre is trying to find me, but he will not be able to find me because it is much deeper than you may know. Once everything is over, I will tell you everything but right now is not the best time to tell you because I do not know who is watching. Kiss my kids for me and keep them safe I know you will keep them safe. Love you Niya That was the letter that was it and that was all. She did not leave a return address or tell me about her case. I was starting to doubt that Niya was in jail since we had not found her yet. This was so strange. Niya called that first day and she called to make sure I had her kids. After that the calls were just a few seconds letting me know that she was okay. I did not know what she was saying about Hakeem I thought he was a pretty okay guy. Niya was a woman with many secrets though. She did tell me that he used hit her though, maybe that is what she meant. We had not seen each other since Niya's honeymoon. I would try to connect with her but Niya was always too busy. She had left me in control of her companies, and I would deposit her money right into her account that was her portion. Niya had other businesses that she was into. I did not know what they were because I had my hands full with the ones, she had left me in charge of. I did not know that being a businesswoman could be so hard thankfully I was born into the business. I had gotten advice from my father who owned hotels across the county. My big sister Monica also was a businesswoman in Michigan. Other than Niya, Monica was my best friend who I talked about everything with. I had told my sister certain things about Niya but I really did not have anything to go off of. Monica had been telling me for years that girl is dangerous. I didn't know how true that was. All the years we had known each other, and I knew so little about my friend. I felt special because she felt safe enough to leave her kid's in my custody, so I knew that Niya loved and respected me, but she was just so private. It also made me wonder with Niya being so private what else was she hiding though. To just up and call me and break some news to me about killing Rashad that was just crazy. The chills ran up my spine to even think that Niya could be capable of something like murder. My father was another special part of my life he made it so that we would be well taken care of. Before I started working for Niya I was just a receptionist and although I liked my job to be the boss was something new to me. Yes, I could have helped my father with his business, but I wanted to branch off and do my own thing and I was happy that Niya had trusted me so much. I did not know what that letter meant but I was going to show Tre. I went to the other bedroom where Malcolm and Deena slept. They had to share rooms because Tre and I only had a two-bedroom home. I saw that they were still awake, and I went to tell them that I had contact with their mother. Even if it was just a letter something was better than nothing. "Malcolm, Deena I got a letter from your Mom." I had not really asked them about the events that took place because I did not know what to say. I did not know if they saw their Mom kill their stepfather or what. "She doing okay?" Malcolm asked. I felt bad for the kids. They had lost their father and now they may lose their mother. "Yes, she fine honey she did not tell me much about what was going on, but she did say she was okay." "Oh, I know what is going on. I just wanted to make sure she was okay." He said. I looked at him in surprise. "Well what is going on?" I wanted to know. Malcolm looked up at the wall. He was becoming quite a handsome young man. He looked a lot like his father. "A lot but Mama said she would explain everything to you." That is what he said but I could tell it was something else to what he was saying but I could not read between the lines. I needed to talk to Tre. That night Tre made it home around two and he woke me up when he got in the bed. I was restless anyway, so it was easy for him to stir me. He put his arms around my waist, and I turned towards him. I kissed his nose and he smiled. "Baby Niya wrote me a letter but she did not leave a return address." "What you mean?" He asked getting excited. "She did not leave a return address." I repeated it again. Tre jumped up. "Let me see the letter." Although Tre was exhausted, he jumped back on to the scene like he was at work. He got up early at six in the morning and went to work every morning. People would think that I would be tripping not to see my man all day and half of the night, but I understood he was out making money. I got up and went to the drawer and pulled the letter out. I handed it to Tre, and he looked at the envelope. It was a regular envelope and it looked normal, but he noticed one thing that I had not noticed. "Babe where did you get this letter?" "The mailbox what you mean she mailed it to me you see it's in an envelope." "How when there is no stamp on the envelope" He said and showed me the envelope...........

Tre Mya was acting stupid as hell. I know damn well she knew this envelope did not have a damn stamp on it. Her pretty ass just sitting here with her hair all wild and looking at me like I was crazy. One thing I loved about Mya was that she was naïve. It was cute and I adored her. I had been dating her for five years and I had fallen in love with this woman. I know a man like me is not supposed to fall in love, but I had and as much as I hated to lie to her I did it every single day. I told Mya that I am a private investigator and that is true for the most part but when I find my, target I kill them. I am a hired hitman and I am good at my job. I am one of the most top paid hitmen. It hurts me to pretend to be broke for Mya. The truth is it also makes me feel good that she is not dating me for my money but because she actually loves me. To be honest I love everything about the woman. That crazy ass wild hair of hers, the fact that she doesn't nag me, the way she keeps my food warm no matter how late I come home. She loves me and I love her but this friend of hers, Aniya she is all trouble. Ever since I met Mya, Aniya has had problem after problem. I know everything even though she does not know I know. I know about the suspicious death of her baby daddy Hakeem. Bruce, I have my own suspicions just because they were having so many problems and then BAM the nigga is dead. Plus, I know that her husband Rashad ain't shit. She thinks he is hot shit, but that nigga is dangerous. I don't know what it is about Aniya but from one killer to the next I know that she is a killer. She hides it well and she is remarkable at killing without a trace. Now this bitch has disappeared, and I can't even find her. I have everybody on this shit, and we cannot find her that can only mean one thing she is working with the Feds. In that case I can't even touch that. I do my dirty work with the local police I ain't that stupid to get twisted with the Feds. I could see the worry on my lady's face, and I wanted to make it right. I grabbed Mya and held her. She pushed away from me. I knew what that meant she was worried so that meant I had to really come up with some way to get her distracted, but I just did not know how. From day one I had been there trying to win Mya's heart. I think I did that when I kept helping her out with Aniya's problems. These five years with her moving to Atlanta was the best. I knew her husband was selling drugs for some Mexican Al

Richards. I did not know everything that was going on, but I knew that much. I was happy that Aniya had left us alone. Mya wanted to know why her friend had changed on her. I told her that she was enjoying her marriage and to leave it like that. Honestly, I was happy though she was too many problems. Now here she was five years later causing more problems and once again we had her kids.

Chapter Three
MYA

I had tossed and turned that entire night. I still did not have any answers for what I had learned. How the hell can an envelope be mailed without a stamp? It couldn't so that meant that someone dropped it off to me but whom? I had not heard anyone in the driveway, and I did not hear a car so who could have delivered it? Niya was supposed to be in jail so who could deliver it? This had my head all messed up. All day I tried to busy myself with work, but I was dragging and not focused at all. My mind kept going back to the letter and I wanted answers I felt that I was owed that much. I called Tre at work to see if he could give me some answers. He still did not know what was going on and he had taken the letter to work with him. I decided to get my mind off the mystery because truth be told I could not do anything about it. I asked Deena if she wanted to come with me and go to the nail shop. Malcolm said he wanted to stay behind so I told him that it would be okay. He was old enough and he was going to stay in the house. Deena and I had a great time. I really did enjoy spending time with my Goddaughter especially since I could not have any kids of my own. It hurt when I thought about it, but I knew that it was meant to be. Everyone did not need a child sometimes that was not what life had in store for them. I knew that one day I would be blessed with the life that I wanted and needed. I knew that it was near. After years of dealing with Chris's bullshit and his baby mama drama I was happy that I was free to do as I pleased. Tre was everything I was looking for. Sometimes I was upset because he worked long hours, but he always came home to me one thing Chris never had done. Chris at first was a sweet guy we had been dating since High School. He was a tall blonde white guy and he was awesome just as much as he was handsome. He was a fun guy to be around and when I found that the popular guy in school was into me it made my heart flutter. I could still feel the way my stomach fluttered when Niya came up to me and told me that Chris liked me. I had just finished my fifth period class and was waiting for Niya to come to our lockers that we shared so that we could enjoy lunch together. I had my hair in a cute bun on top of my head. My sister Monica had flattened my hair and my long, curly hair had transformed into some long, straight hair that went to my butt. Niya came up to me with a scrunched face that looked like she was annoyed. Niya had gotten bigger since Middle School. All the guys looked at her butt and talked about how big her butt was. I thought my friend was coming to tell me about another perverted guy. "Girl guess who like you?" In an aggravated tone. "Who?" I asked feeling excited since we had started High School two years ago. I had not had a boyfriend. Niya had one boyfriend who she kept saying was not her boyfriend, but they were always with each other. "Chris ugh" Niya rolled her eyes to show her hatred for him. "Really?" I had a secret crush on the guy who Niya did not like. Niya said that Chris was a jerk, but she didn't even know him. "Ugh girl you like him too" Niya said laughing and I smiled. "I guess I will give him your number since you crushing on his big head ass too." After that everything was history from there Niya eventually started liking Chris because at first, he treated me so sweet. After High School we made our life together well we were supposed to. So, when he started cheating it was so confusing and it hurt me something awful. Everytime I called Niya she was there to hear my problems. Niya never judged she just listened. Niya did not like Chris after she heard that he cheated on me, but she never told me I should leave. It was my decision Niya was just there to listen. That was what a best friend was supposed to do not judge but listen. So now that Aniya was having problems I was there to listen and to help in any way. A favor for a favor. Niya never talked about anything that she was going through in her life. I actually loved the last couple of months before she got married because Niya was very open and I got to see my friend in action. Niya was so smart, sassy, and in a way conniving. Although we all make mistakes in life it was like Niya would crisscross through every obstacle and zigzag into her destiny. She was strong and I loved that about her. When she got married and became distant, I just did not understand. I had hoped everything was okay and although we had the casual conversations about the business and money, we never talked like we had before I truly missed my best friend. When I got the call that Niya was in jail it scared me because I really was worried about my friend. When Deena and I made it back to the house I called out to Malcolm. I had bought some Popeye's

Chicken on the way from the salon and I was starving. Deena had been quiet most of the time when we were gone. I was trying to get some information out of the little girl but the harder I tried the quieter she got. I told Deena to go upstairs and get her brother. "Malcolm not upstairs" Deena came back downstairs and said to me, I was confused. "What you mean he not upstairs?" I asked as I pulled the chicken out of the bag. "He not up there he gone." Deena said and I dropped the coleslaw on the floor and ran up the stairs. I screamed out Malcolm's name and didn't get an answer. I ran to his room and he was not in there. I ran to the bathroom and he was not in there. I was sweating and panicking, and my curly hair was all over my head. I called Tre and he didn't answer I didn't know what to do. I went back into the room that the kids shared and sat on the bed that belonged to Malcolm. I sat in total shock, where was he? There was no trace of any one being in the house. I could not believe that the boy was gone. I should have never left him alone. I did not know what was going on, but I ran downstairs to make sure Deena was there. Deena was sitting at the table eating her food. "Did you find Malcolm?" She asked through bites. I looked at her beautiful face with her curly long hair she kind of reminded me of me when I was little. "Yeah he okay honey." "Mama must have came to get him while we were gone." I just looked at the little girl. I did not know what to say I did not know how to tell her that her brother was taken, and it was my fault for leaving him alone. I plopped down next to Deena, but I did not eat. I was too worried. I wish I had not gotten my nails done because I wanted to bite on them nails so bad. After Deena got finished eating, we went into the living room to watch television. My mind was not there. As she laughed at Patrick and Spongebob, I sat there crying inside I had fucked up. Tre still had not called me back and I did not know if I should call the police or what I should do. I was just going to sit and wait to see what was going on because I was scared and puzzled. The butterflies in my stomach were not helping and I felt as if I was going to be sick. Niya had trusted me with her most precious gifts and I had been stupid enough to let them out of my sight. I felt that Malcolm was old enough to watch himself but what I didn't know was that someone was watching him. This upset me that someone could come in my house where I was supposed to feel safe and take him out of there. And why the fuck had Tre not called me back? Did they not know that my fiancée was a private investigator who worked for the police? Obviously, whoever it was didn't care. I had fallen asleep in the room with Deena because I was scared that Deena would come up missing too. I felt Tre tugging at me in the middle of the night. Tired and baffled I walked into the room with him. "Where Malcolm at?" He asked pulling off his work shirt. "I don't know." I was still a bit sleep. "What you mean you don't know?" He walked up to me and gave me a kiss. "Somebody took him" I cried as it hit me all at once I had lost Malcolm it was too much for me. "What you mean somebody took him? Took him from where?" Tre voice had gotten loud. "I called you and you did not answer, and you did not call me back. When Deena and I went to the nail shop… when we came back, he was gone." I cried I was now fully awake. "Why didn't you call the police or anything. I would have gotten that call." Tre screamed and walked towards his shirt. "I was waiting for you to call me back!" I screamed. "Bullshit Mya! You know what is going on here you better tell me more because this shit don't make sense. You call me for everything else and you won't call me for something serious like your best friend son coming up missing? What the fuck that don't sound right! How did the person get in?" Tre screamed you could tell that he was noticeably angry. He had never yelled at me and he had never had a reason too. "Are you trying to say that I had something to do with this? You fucking asshole he's my Godson! I don't know how they got in." I stormed out the room and went back to sleep in the kids' room. I was upset and I did not know how Tre could accuse me of making my own Godson disappear. I sat and thought about it for a minute. No, I did not call the police when I should have but I was scared because I really did not know what to do. All this mysterious bullshit was new to me. All this was new to me I had grown up sheltered and loved. I did not know what to do with missing children and best friends being in jail. I started crying again I could not believe I had let this happen. I heard Tre come into the room. He was by the doorway. "I am sorry okay. I just don't understand why you wouldn't think this is urgent? You have to think Mya this shit is serious." I knew that I wasn't a kid. "It's bad already that no one can find Niya and every time I call the Atlanta Police department, I am not getting any information. You say she is in jail? But no one can find her. You need to think really hard because we need answers because now her son is missing, and they want to know where she is. Who can help us out?" Huh he was getting on my nerves hell he was the damn investigator. I had not been close to Niya in five years. Out of the blue she calls me and tells me that she killed her husband and that I need to get my God kids. I did not know what the hell was going on, but everything was getting on my nerves already. I did not know what to do or how to handle this situation. I was used to a quiet lifestyle except for the dumb relationships I had ended up in. But Tre was right I was in the middle of it so it was time to think. Who could we call to see what might have happened? Who did I know that Niya knew? Damn no one. Niya's mother was dead, she didn't know her father, and Rashad's brother was dead oh wait. "Rebeccca!" I screamed. We had gone to Chicago and met Bruce and Rashad's sister Rebecca before. "Yeah pack your shit we going to Chicago." Tre said.

Tre I really needed to find this bitch Niya and quick. She was turning my world upside down. I had been looking for her everywhere. I mean I didn't know the chick like that, but I know she was my woman's best friend. Mya was not letting me touch her ever since them kids moved in. From day one I treated Malcolm and Deena like my own they were easy to love. Malcolm was smart. One day he may be a trained killer if he stuck around me. Deena she was quiet a princess. She was the type of girl that you just wanted to protect. Those beautiful hazel eyes just made her much more innocent. I wanted to find their mother to help these kids. I was a killer no lie, but I had a heart. Everything about me was not just kill, kill, kill. I loved Mya she was the closest thing I had to family and her family accept me. I loved every bit of it. Her sister Monica was sweet, Monica's husband Joey was a real cool dude too, straight square. I didn't have anyone but my brother Ken. He was all that I had left. He was everything to me. Niya had even hired him as a manager for her companies. I loved that so I was going to take the extra time to find her. Once Malcolm disappeared, I got worried. I didn't mean to snap at Mya, but she was acting stupid as hell. Like come on this shit is serious and you didn't think to call me. I need for her to have her head on straight. This shit is serious. Then on top of that someone broke into our home and took Malcolm. Niggas knew who I was in this area, so I knew it wasn't a person from here. They left no trace too. I mean they went in and out in no time. I even checked the locks there were little scratch marks, but the lock was not damaged whoever this guy was he was good. I was happy that Mya had finally used that pretty head of hers for not just looking cute and to actually think. Rebecca, I knew for a fact that she was married to Rashad's brother on his mother's side Darien. She might be the key to everything. I thought that it was sick for them to be married but whatever floats their boats. Rebecca had told us a sick ass story about their brother Bruce. I know Aniya felt stupid as hell she was sleeping with that white boy and he was foul. I was laughing inside at her ass. I loved Mya but Aniya was fine as hell. She needed her a nigga that white boy didn't know what to do with all those curves. Mya is skinny and fit while Aniya got a fat ass. I mean you can't help but too look. When I met Mya, I was checking out the both of them really. So, when she Mya gave me the go ahead, I went for her. It was just something about the way she looked so innocent and pure. She had to be mine. I was happy that she was the one who came to talk to me. The way bodies were dropping around Aniya I might had been next. Mya was the perfect one for me. As soon as I figure all this shit out, I am going to marry that woman.

Chapter Four

MYA

⟫⟫⟩⟩⟨⟨⟨⟨

We headed out that night and went to Chicago. Tre was flying like a bat out of hell and was making all types of calls. I was hoping that Rebecca still lived in the same house that we had visited five years ago. We had gone to Rebecca's house to find out information on Niya's boyfriend Bruce at the time. Rebecca was Bruce's sister and when she had told us what he had done to her it was unbelievable. He had betrayed his sister in the worst way, and it was disgusting. Bruce had his own issues that he needed to deal with so when he killed himself it was no surprise to. I could not fathom how he had tolerated himself for that long. I remembered the day that we had gone to Chicago to talk to Rebecca. I had taken the kids in the kitchen so that they could not hear the adults talking. I listened by the door of the kitchen at the gruesome details. That day would forever haunt me. I had blocked the thoughts out of my head I could not believe that someone could do that to their sister. Before I knew it, I had tears falling from my eyes. Malcolm was about five then and he came up to me and hugged me. I knew that he must have seen his mother crying before because he knew how to comfort, and he knew what being sad was. When we pulled up to the big house it was light outside, but the house was dark. Tre told me to stay put because Deena was still in the car sleep. I did not want to hear that, so I woke the child up and proceeded to the house by his side. Tre knocked and called Rebecca's name. There was no answer. He tried the knob and surprisingly it was unlocked he pulled out his pistol and proceeded in the house with Deena and I behind him. He told us to be quiet. The house was eerily quiet and astonishingly clean. It was like no one had lived in the house for months. Tre told us to sit downstairs while he searched the big house. I was scared for him, but I stayed put in the living room where I hugged a shaken Deena. I was afraid myself, but I was not going to let Deena see that. I did not know how to tell the girl that her brother was missing and honestly so was her mother. After about ten minutes I got tired of waiting not tired of waiting but I was becoming afraid, so I was about to go search for Tre when the telephone rang. It blared so loud because the house was so quiet. I jumped and looked at the phone and saw that it was a private number. I was not the nosey type, but something made me pick up this call. "Hello," I said. "Rebecca?" It was Niya she was calling straight through this was not a jail call. "Niya it's me Mya" I said quickly "what is going on I thought you was in jail?" "Damn girl what you doing in Rebecca's house?" Just then Tre walked up to me. "What is going on Niya! Malcolm is missing!" I yelled. "He's not missing he is safe don't listen to nothing anyone tells you I will be writing you." Niya hung up and all I heard was a click. "What the fuck she say?" Tre asked. "She said that Malcolm is safe and not to believe anything anyone tells me." I was confused and the riddles were making my head hurt what the hell was going on? "Man, what the hell is going on?" Tre asked to no one in particular. As we headed back to his truck. We had a long ride home. We were both silent wasn't anything to say since we didn't know what was going on. Once we made it home there was another letter in the mailbox without a return address. Deena went upstairs to take a nap and Tre and I sat down together and read the letter. Dear Mya, I know you worried about me, but I am okay. Malcolm was taken but he is with me we had to make it seem like he was kidnapped in order for him to disappear without a trace. We have not talked in a long time and to be honest you do not know what my life consists of now. Deena will disappear soon too so don't beat yourself up about it they are safely with me. It's just that I could not take them with me at the time. My life has been rough there are things that you do not know about me Mya and there are things that I need to tell you. Just so that you can understand what I have been through to get to this point. Hakeem was my first love and he rescued me from abuse and rape. When I lived with my mother her boyfriend James was raping me and forcing me to be with him. Every time you and I would go out and I would get that call that would be James dirty ass. I told you it was not what you thought. Yes, his dirty ass was having sex with my mom and me at the same time. You don't know how many times I scrubbed my body clean just thinking about the dirty bastard. I hated him and I hated my mother. He beat me up and strangled me until I had sex with him. I lived in total fear for a year and a half and my Mother did not do anything about it. She knew what the hell was going on, but it was like she didn't care. The day that

Hakeem made me go get my clothes from her house was the day that I found out my mother was on drugs. All those years and I didn't notice. I don't know how that shit flew over my head and it still don't make any sense. Hell, it is a lot of people on drugs who would not allow their kids to be raped. I know I was an adult but that do not make it right. That shit fucked up my head because he was raping me, but I liked the way his sex felt. I mean what woman wouldn't like a tongue being on her clitoris just the right way. And although he was rough it turned me on while turning me off at the same way. It was conflicting that was for sure. Still to this day I am confused with not just myself but my mother as well. I assume that my Mother was doing drugs and she fell into debt with James and she told him that he could have his way with me. But what she failed to realize was that I was a person too. Not just a person but her daughter her flesh and blood who she had carried in her womb for nine months. I know the love of a mother to a child felt shit I got two. Sadly, I will never know the love from a child to their mother because I never had a mother. To top it off shit that wasn't the first time she had allowed a man to molest me. Mr. Jones dirty ass I am convinced that she knew about the molestation. Fuck that all those years I was saying to myself no she couldn't have known. She knew just like she knew with James. It didn't matter that I was twenty-two years old the thing about it is that it was not right. I was afraid to go home, and I was embarrassed. I did not know what being in love was until I met Hakeem. Not just love from a man but love period. I did not have that I did not have a mother/daughter relationship with my mother was. She never told me she loved me and when she killed herself, I wanted to amend things, but I couldn't. I found her dead in her bathtub when I was pregnant with Malcolm. The shit hurt my heart. Not because she was dead no at first, I thought that you know the grievance of all people who lose their mothers. But I know why I was so hurt. It was because she had failed to even explain why she did not care about me. She failed to explain why she had left me out to rot and be used and abused. She had failed at the one thing in life that was truly important being my mother. Who could do such a thing? Okay this shit is getting to me I will write soon stop worrying. Love you Aniya There was tears stains on the paper when I got done reading, I could not believe all the things that Niya was telling me. Tre was silent and so was I. I had known Niya since we were young teenagers and I could not even imagine that she was going through that shit. I did remember before she met Hakeem how her phone would ring and all of a sudden she would have to leave. I thought that Niya was being private about her life and she was, but she had good reason too. That night I lay in Tre's arms and thought about all the things that Niya had been through. All these things were going on right up under my nose and I had no idea. What else was she hiding from me? This was just the icing on the cake, and you could tell. The last five years I did not know what Aniya had gotten herself into, but I surely wanted to find out but was it even worth it? Although I worried about Aniya apparently, she could take care of herself. She had been doing well for herself all these years. I was worried about Malcolm though and I was definitely worried about Deena disappearing. I did not know if this was the right thing and what was going on, but she was their mother. I couldn't do anything but let everything take place I had no say so in what was going to happen.

Tre When we went to Chicago, I had left Mya downstairs with A'Deena while I looked around upstairs. Everything was gone. I thought I was going to run into some trouble because I had heard of Rashad's brother Darien but wasn't any clothes or anything in that house. I looked in every room in that big ass house and nothing. I heard the phone ringing and raced downstairs. Mya had answered it and said that it was Niya. Niya had told her that the girl would be disappearing too. I did not know what the fuck was going on, but I was tired of the games. I wasn't getting paid for this shit and to be honest I had other shit to do. I had a job that I had to do, and I needed to complete that instead of worrying about Niya. She would show up one day.I got up the next morning and headed to my office. When I got in the office, I had a note on my desk. It had a number on it. I called it. "Hello." "Yeah who this?" The voice sounded familiar, but I could not place it. "The Reaper." "Damn nigga what up?" I asked him. "Shit a lot you know Aniya?" "Yeah, yeah, that is my girl's best friend." It looked like I was finally going to get some answers. I knew I would get some information on Aniya I just didn't think it would be coming from him. "What you know about her?" The Grim Reaper asked. "Shit nothing really the bitch got bread, companies, she got two kids why what's up?" I couldn't let him know too much before I found out what he knew. "Nothing I just been hearing talk about her." "You know where she at?" I knew that nigga knew more. "Maybe." This nigga was being too vague for me. He was making me mad. Something told me he knew where she was. I didn't know what was going on so I told him the only thing I knew that would make my wife happy. "Keep her safe." "Alright." He answered. I hung up. I didn't know what Aniya had gotten herself into, but I know that her and her kids would be safe if The Reaper protected them. He had worked for me at one point and time and the man was good, but he had a heart, so I let him go before he got into deep. He was a killer, but he wasn't an assassin it wasn't something he could do for life. I relaxed a bit. I was worried about the lady and her kids, but she had too much hidden. I wanted Mya to stop stressing and that was the only reason why I even cared what happened to her. I know it would have hurt Mya too bad and I did not like to see my little lady cry. I looked at Mya's picture on my desk. I smiled at her. She was so beautiful with those pink lips. I smiled she was way different than my ex-wife. I shook my head I didn't want to think about that bitch. My phone rung and it was back to business I had to get my mind right. It was time to clean the city up.

Chapter Five
MYA

⟶ ◦ ⟫⟩﷽⟨⟨ ◦ ⟵

The thought of A'Deena disappearing came and stayed until the week she disappeared. I was an emotional mess since we were staying in the house and Deena was starting to ask questions. I knew the girl wanted answers because her brother had disappeared so suddenly. She was young but she was not stupid she knew something was going on. I did not have any answers for the young girl, so I tried to avoid the conversation. Tre was trying his hardest to figure out what was going on, but he was at a dead end also. I told Deena to get herself dressed because we were going to the mall. Deena happily obliged because she was tired of being in the house. I made sure Deena put on bright colors so that she would not get lost in the crowd. It was a Wednesday so I was confident that it would not be a lot of people in the mall. After I had checked on the companies and made sure the books were balanced out correctly, we were off to the mall. I wore some black leggings to show off my toned legs and a white little t shirt. Thank goodness for perfect genes because I hated to workout, but I stayed in shape. Deena was cute in her little yellow sundress and we were good to go. Both of our curly hair was bouncy and full of life and if no one had known that I could not have children they would have thought she was my child. The resemblance was remarkable. I loved the way that people would compliment us in the short time we were together and out. If I had a daughter, then I knew that Deena and my daughter would have similar features. We shopped till we dropped, and Deena was enjoying herself. She kept asking when her Mother was coming to get her. I had told the girl that Malcolm was with their Mother and I did not know how true that was because it was only words. I did not know if those letters were actually from Niya. I did not know if someone was setting her up and that is what worried me. We headed to the Mall's food court. I sat our bags down and told Deena I was going to get us some food. I walked up to the restaurant and I turned back to glance at Deena. When I looked at the area, I had left her at she was gone. I quickly ran over. My bags were still there but I was not crazy Deena was gone. restroom by herself. I turned my head and she was gone. I looked everywhere and I did not find her. I went to the Mall's security to help locate Deena, but she was gone. I did not know what to do. I had lost the kids. Security did not see anything on the cameras unusual. I had no idea what had happened in a blink of an eye the little girl was gone just like Malcolm. But this time Deena was taken right from under my nose. When they contacted the police, I called Tre and he came to the mall. He looked nice as usual in his button-down shirt and I ran to him in tears. "Babe I don't know what happen this time? I turned my head and she was gone." I was in tears. The police had been grilling me and they were really getting on my nerves. They were asking me questions that had nothing to do with Deena coming up missing. Like if I was intoxicated or on drugs. I guess they just wanted to make sure this was not a fake story since the security cameras hadn't captured Deena with me. All the cameras showed Deena steps behind me and it did make it seem like she was not with me. The only thing that really led them to believe that we were together was the outside cameras when we got out the car. I don't know why but there were no cameras in the food court. It was just unbelievable no one at the mall seemed to know that she was taken. I felt like I was in a dream Tre took me home and when he went into the mailbox there was another letter to me. He threw the letter on the bed. "This is from Niya I bet. What the fuck is she doing? Why the fuck is she putting you through this bullshit?" He snapped. He was visibly pissed, and I was in agreement. Why was my "best friend" doing this to me? Why did she allow the kids to come with me and then they disappear without a trace? If that was the case she should have taken them with her in the first place. I tore the letter open. Dear Mya, Thanks for getting the kids for me. I have them both now. Don't be mad I just needed people to think that my kids were not with me. It is so much to explain right now because to be honest I do not know what is going on. I just do as they tell me and try to keep myself as sane as possible. I will try to keep in touch. Love you A'Niya P.S. Tell Tre to stop trying to look for me he do, not need to uncover this shit. I read it out loud, so Tre heard what she wrote. "Damn what the fuck is she into?" Tre said. I did not know what Aniya was into, but I was tired. It seemed like the only time she was around me was when she needed some help. She needed our help to figure out all that shit with Bruce,

Quita, and Cedes and now she was in some type of trouble and was spoon feeding us information. I did not know what was going on and I did not care to know now. I was fed up and I was happy the kids were gone because now I could live my life and get things back to normal if she needed me Aniya knew where to find me.

Tre I did not know what Aniya was into, but I know she had the Feds working with her. The Reaper had called me, and I really wanted to know what he knew. I knew for a fact that The Reaper worked for his Uncle Al Richards. Al Richards was a scum. He would kill anything moving. His organization used to be large, but it had gotten small ever since he decided to kill his associates. He was free lancing for people to push weight for him. No one really knew that his organization had downgraded but I knew for sure he had killed most of the people who worked for him. I had heard that Rashad was running drugs for him but when I told Mya to invite Niya so that I could question her she never came. I wanted to warn her Al Richards did not give a fuck he knew every criminal there was. From prostitution, to drugs, to robbery he did it all. He didn't do as much as he used to because he had killed off so many branches of his organization. Al Richards was going to be put under the jail if they found the right person to testify against him. That was hard because every time he was up for trial the witness would be killed or disappear. I really did not care one-way or another. If something happened to Niya that was on her. But I did care about her kids and I know my wife would have been angry with me if I didn't help in some type of way. I was pissed when I found out that Deena was missing. That was my little princess she was beautiful just like my wife. I was mad but at the same time I knew that if her Mother was working with the Feds then the kids were in good hands. I just hoped like hell everything was going to be okay from now on because it was time for Mya and I to move on with our life. After I made sure Mya was straight at home, I made my way to the bank. I had millions in my account, and I was tired of hiding it. I knew that Mya was with me because she wanted to be, and she had no hidden agendas. I took out some cash so I could go buy the ring that I wanted to give Mya. As I walked into Kay Jewelers, I smiled I could not believe I was ready to get married again. I knew that Mya was the right one for me. I just hoped that all my secrets would stay hidden and that we would live happily ever after.

Chapter Six
ANIYA

I lay on my bed with my kids and I was at peace. Finally, I had them back in my arms. I was still a bit afraid, but I knew that I was protected. Deena and Malcolm were so happy to see me, and I was happy to see them. I had not seen them since the FEDS came to get me from the hotel. Rashad and I had the perfect marriage on the outside. We were racking in money like a muthafucka and we were Atlanta's Beyonce and Jay-Z as far as we were concerned. Mya was holding it down for me and sending me fat ass checks from all my companies up North. I loved being a businesswoman, but Rashad wanted to expand and not legally. Mr. Richards the guy who we had bought the strip club from he was a drug dealer the rumors were true. Mr. and Mrs. Thompson knew him, and Rashad wanted to start expanding his business. I was the key to the operation. I would transport the drugs to different dealers around Atlanta. Mr. Richards believed in Rashad and because he could not sell the dope himself, he put it up to Rashad. Basically Mr. Richards was the plug, but Rashad was pretending as if he was. Rashad did not know why Mr. Richards wanted it to be like he was the front runner but that was the plan. After the first year his brother Darien got out of jail and him and Rebecca helped a lot. We got some clientele in Chicago as well. Rebecca had been willing and dealing and handling shit for Darien while he was locked up. So, she had developed a rapport with the drug dealers in Chicago. Darien got out of jail at the end of the year it was sort of cold outside. I remember thinking I hope it don't snow in the South. When it snows down south everything shuts down and I was not in the mood to be on stand still. I had a party to throw and I was ready to finally meet my brother in law. Rebecca and I had met before and Darien did not want her to go to work for Rashad until he knew everything was everything. He knew about Mr. Richards and he wanted to make sure the deal was on the up and up. Darien had gotten out of jail that Monday and they were flying in today. Rashad came in the kitchen and checked to make sure everything was good. He looked at the cook I had hired. She was a student at the college that was going to culinary school. She was a young Philippine with long black hair. She stood about five foot one and she was cute with her little glasses. She was very respectable, and she did her job well. I could tell that she was going to be successful. He tested out the chocolate dessert that was prepared and moaned from how good it was. "That shit is delicious." He said as he gave me a kiss on my cheek. "Baby those niggas gone love this shit." He laughed. It was going to be a small gathering because Darien didn't like too many people. It was going to be Rashad and I, Rebecca and Darien, their little sister Elise and her husband Dewayne, their cousin Terrel and his lady Melody. So, it was going to be intimate. Plus, I did not like a lot of people knowing where we lived knowing the illegal business, we were doing you had to be careful. I had told the kids to stay upstairs because it was going to be a grown folks party by eight o'clock they both had drifted off to sleep. Ever since we had moved into this big ass house the kids had stayed in the room together because they both were afraid to sleep alone. Darien and Rebecca had been in the city for a couple hours now and Rebecca had him up shopping and getting him clean for the party.

I was a bit nervous I had not met Darien. As much as Rashad talked about his brother I really wanted to impress him. I had gotten my hair done and I really liked the all black Peruvian weave with the part in the middle. It was straight and the inches were fierce twenty-four inches I was definitely feeling good. Rashad kept complimenting my hair and I was smiling from ear to ear. The man had definitely been a God send. He had shown me how to make money legally and illegal. I was rolling in dough that money I had spent for the house I had got that back and I was still in had millions in my bank account. Rashad had his own bank account and it was damn near close to mine, but I had him beat. He gave me a cut of the drug money since I was the mule. I was making money but to be honest this last year was exhausting. I was running around town so much I barely had time to really spend with the children. Rashad was definitely good in that area. He took Malcolm to baseball, football, soccer, hell and whatever else sport he played. Deena was my little ballerina and cheerleader. Malcolm had grown fond of Rashad and they both referred to him as Daddy Shad. They loved him and that made me love him even more. Sometimes Rashad would make the runs but most of all I was the one who did the drug running. It was fun too. Mr. and Mrs. Thompson were initially the boss when it came to the negotiation. The first year was great Mr. Richards delivered on time and everything was smooth. Over time though he started fucking up. It was a Monday and we only had three people that we sold too at the time and they were money makers. We did not sell lightweight so Mr. Richards delivering the product was crucial to being on time. I had called him that night to let him know how much we would need, and he said he could deliver that morning. That morning at nine am he was not even answering his phone for me. I called Mr. Thompson and he gave him a ring. He answered and told him it would be noon. I had to call the clientele back and tell them two when at first it was noon. When noon came, I called Mr. Richards and again he gave me a different time. Now anybody knows even in the drug game that you do not change times. That shit made it seem like you were setting muthafuckas up and that was a death sentence. Rashad called his Dad and his Dad called Mr. Richards and the old man gave him the run around. Rashad said fuck that. He went to the old man house and made him deliver. I don't know what he did, but he left with the delivery. We were on a time frame and this shit was not a game. Do you know what they do to muthafuckas who they thought was planning and plotting on them?

These were some real niggas. They were about their fucking money and I did not know what they did to get all that dough, but we needed it and I was not going to die to get it. That day Rashad made the drop offs because he did not want to put me in danger. He even gave the guys a onetime discount because he wanted to make sure we were in good standing. He did the next three drop offs just to make sure I was not in any danger and that the guys were okay. That was just the beginning we started off with three and now years later we were selling too several different guys in Chicago and Atlanta. Terrel and his lady Melody arrived at the party first. Terrel was a dusty looking cat who came up on some dough when Rashad put him on. He was paying us back at that time because he didn't have enough money to start slanging such large amounts of dope. Rashad looked out and Terrel was a true bonefide hustler. He came up and he got him a bad ass Puerto Rican chick named Melody. Melody was a drug runner like me. We hustled with our men. I loved the power of knowing that I was supplying, and I was a boss. Not only was I a boss in the board room but I was a boss on the streets. Elise was a new face for me her and her guy Dewayne. I had seen her on pictures, but this was my first time seeing her in person. Her husband was a drunk, so Elise pretty much ran things. She was not like her sister Rebecca. Elise was a thick white chick with a black girl ass. She had red hair and a ghetto girl attitude. Rebecca was a beauty queen with a little slim waist and big titties. Elise was stunning too but she was just a different stunning. Rebecca had the personality of a woman who was in charge because she had grace, but Elise demanded power because she was outspoken and a real go getter. She had not been doing any drug running yet but Rashad was planning on sending her out because he did not trust Dewayne. Darien and Rebecca made their grand entrance and I must say Darien was fine. He was another type of fine but him and Rebecca was definitely made for each other. Darien was buff and built and he looked about 6' 2. He had deep waves in his hair, and he was the color of Hershey's chocolate. My mouth stood open I was definitely thinking this man was fine and I could tell why Rebecca rode those three years with him he was definitely worth waiting for. He hugged Elise and gave Dewayne a handshake. He walked over to Terrel and gave him a handshake and he gave Melody a hug. I could tell by the way he looked at Melody he definitely liked her. He came over to Rashad and I and gave his brother a strong embrace you could tell they were really close. "This my wife Aniya" Rashad said pushing me forward. He smiled at me and gave me a hug. "Damn you smell good" he said after he let me go. "What is that?" I laughed "sweat shit I'm so nervous about meeting you." He laughed "ain't no reason to be nervous about meeting me we gone get along fine my sistah." And it was true Darien and I got along great when we saw each other. We had met up a couple of times on business and for family gatherings and Darien always treated me like a sister. I had noticed a couple of times he eyed me in a sexual way, but he never made any advances. He was the life of the party and kept us laughing. We were drinking, eating, talking shit, and shooting pool. I was having the best time of my life and I was happy that I had met Rashad. He kept me smiling. We had some occasional arguments but that was to be expected. I loved this man and his family. They had welcomed me with open arms sometimes I wonder if they liked me because they all knew I killed Bruce. I know that Rashad knew but I wonder if he had told anyone. They did not like Bruce because of the downfall and suffering he had cost their family, but I always wondered what did they really think of me? At first his mother was distant but that was nothing that didn't change with time. Damn I was going to miss her. Mr. and Mrs. Thompson had moved out of the country before any of this happened.

Mrs. Thompson had done a lot for me and the kids and she was the closest thing I had to a mother. She would watch the kids for me and when Rashad and I had problems I knew that I could talk with her. She would not just side with her son. She would take the time to listen and actually give me good advice. You just don't know how many times I came to her door crying over her son. When he started cheating, I wanted to leave but I honestly loved him. I loved what we had become. I was not the type of woman to just quit a relationship because things weren't going my way. I had learned that with Hakeem. If I could endure that abuse for five years, then I could try to make things work with a man who committed his life to me. I was going to miss those talks though. The day that she told us they were leaving to go out the country I was devastated. They had come up on a little dough and left. I did not know where they were, but I think that they knew all of this was going to happen they had just left a week before I killed Rashad. All of this shit just had to happen and now I had to be without the one I loved. Damn I hated the way that things had to end. I really loved that man and it hurt me to be the one to end his life, but I had had enough. Shit with the lifestyle we lived it was only a matter of time before he ended up dead or in jail. I just didn't think that I would be the one to do it. I wrapped my arms around Malcolm and Deena and was so thankful that I still had them. They felt so warm and soft near me they were my angels I loved them so much. Tears welled up in my eyes and my heart hurt. I had been through so much and I was hoping that it would soon be over. I was in a hard situation that I did not want to be a part of. I did hate the way that I had to trick Mya, but it was the best for my kids. The plan was for her to keep the kids but once I found out that I could have them with me I wanted to make sure that no one knew where they were going. I did not know if they had phones tapped or anything and I did not know if Tre would tell anyone if I just came to get them. The detective said it would be easier this way. We had to make it look like they went missing without a trace like they never existed. I had cried myself to sleep and I was overjoyed when I got my children back, but something was missing. My man Rashad he was missing. All the trips we took, the love we made, the talks we had I missed him, and it was really hurting me to not be with him. But it was my own fault for being so hot headed and not being an adult and talking about my problems. I had done the killing thing so many times that I was starting to think that I was a black widow. The next morning, I made the kids some breakfast. Pancakes, bacon, sausage, grits, eggs, all the things that they liked with a cup of orange juice on the side. I hated this little ass apartment that they had us holed up in. I was hot and it did not make sense I was used to my castle. Dale said that he was going to be back to check on us and I hope that he was going to be killed on the way. I was ready to get this shit over with. I had tried to call Rebecca I just wanted to explain myself about what had happened with her brother. I was shocked to hear Mya answer the phone. I asked Deena when she got to me and she said that Rebecca's house was empty maybe she moved out of the country too. I let the kids go in their room and watch Disney channel because I needed to write Mya. I took out my pen and paper. Dear Mya, I have both my children and thank you for always being there for me. I love you so much and I know that you are worried about us but trust me we are fine. As soon as I figure everything out, I will surely let you know what is going on. I have held so many things back from you. Girl getting beat on by Hakeem was something I was so ashamed of. To actually have to live with a man who I thought loved and rescued me and let him abuse on me. I was trapped though I was too deep in the relationship. Damn all that could have been avoided. Girl I was so damn stupid. I let him take control of all the money. I mean all the money. I let him give me a fucking allowance. Do you believe that shit? Even when my Mother died, I put all the insurance money in his bank account. I can say one thing he did teach me about the business, and he did build companies that took care of me and the kids. Those companies are my life they are like my kids they are everything. I could not believe when I had Bruce as a business partenr and getting a piece of my companies. I trust you and I love you and I know that I can really depend on you that is why I let you get my kids. Sometimes I just sit and wonder why I had the life I had but now I know that it was to make me this strong. I tell you I been through some things and one thing about it is I am proud I overcame the things that I did. Take care of yourself love. Love you, Aniya This was going to be my last letter to Mya I was going to miss my friend, but I had to leave that part of my life alone. I had to move on. I was so anxious for this situation to be over and for my life to move on. I walked into the closet sized room and looked at my children they were at peace. As long as we were together, I knew that they would be okay. They did not have their father but with a father like Hakeem who needed him. Malcolm looked up and smiled at me. "Mama why you crying?" His smile turned into a frown. I didn't even notice I was crying. "I am so happy to have you guys that's why." And that was the truth. I went and got in the bed with them and hugged my children. Damn I was a lucky lady. So much bad shit had happened that I knew all the good that was coming to me was well worth the wait. I had a good life with Rashad but at the same time our life was hard. Not hard like when I was with Hakeem, but it was a different type of hard. I really had to put in work and Rashad really had to make a name out on the streets when it came down to it. No one knew him and that first year was our best year. Terrel was our first client. Then it was this guy he knew Shorty Rob and he was a hustler. But everybody was not on the up and up and we ran into problems with people like Chuck. We were fucking with Chuck the long way, but he kept coming up short. It was like he thought because I was delivering the drugs he could get over. You should have seen the way his eyes lit up when he saw me. I didn't know if he wanted to fuck me or rob me. My guess was rob then fuck me. Well that is exactly what he was doing robbing the shit out of us and fucking us over. He came up short with the money from day one. The first time it was okay, the next time Rashad called and checked him about it, but the third and last time Rashad had to show him he was not be played with.

That was a no, no. Rashad told me baby I will do the runs this time. We never knew when we would have to make runs, we just put a deadline on it and went with it. Chuck, he sold out quick all the time and was short all the time. Chuck was one of those goofy niggas that loved the hustle but felt that everyone owed him something. I don't know exactly what Rashad did to the nigga, but he came back with our cut and the rest of the money that he had been shorting us. After that we didn't have any more dealings with Chuck and my guess is that Chuck went out of business because he never re- up. Life for us was just not the drug game though. We had upgraded the strip club and we owned a little bar. We were not only drug runners, but we were also business folks. Hell, we had our hand in all types of things. I loved that about Rashad he wanted to get it in any way possible. He turned me on to the drug game and to be honest I had loved it at first. It was something different it made my life have a bit of danger in it. But that part of our life had to come to an end. I heard a knock at the door and instantly jumped. I reached for my pistol, but I remembered that I was in witness protection and I did not have a gun. I went to the door. "Who is it?" I heard the familiar voice and opened the door. It was Dale and I was mad that he had made it back to me. His white face was turning red and he had a bald spot on the top of his head. Witness protection my ass. He was not going to save me his old ass could barely see straight. They had to be kidding me. I did not want to be there because I was not a witness to shit. I really did not want to deal with this shit, but it was what I had to do to become a free woman. I felt like this was my only way out of the fucked-up situation I had put myself in.

Chapter Seven
ANIYA

———— ∞◦❧◦❦◦∞ ————

D ale stopped by just to make sure I was still alive. That is it and that is all. I closed the door behind him and went to look for my phone. I had to hide it because no one was supposed to know where the kids and I were at, but one person did. Once I figured out my location, I had made sure to contact Mr. Richards to let him know that I was not going to snitch. He told me that everything would be okay. He was out on bond and I just wanted it all to be over. Truth was I was texting the person who I was supposed to be hiding from. I texted him 'Damn he came back to check on us so when is this going to happen?' I waited for a reply, but I didn't get one. I was tired of sitting in this damn little ass apartment. I had given him the green light since I had gotten Malcolm and Deena back. We were somewhere in Georgia that I knew nothing about. I had overheard Dale telling someone the exact location and when he told them I made sure to tell Mr. Richards. I had to put on a brown wig whenever I went out so that no one would recognize me. I was not supposed to go out at all. Hell, Dale was not watching me 24/7 the shit was not even real witness protection if you ask me because Dale came to check on us once a day and that was it. It was like they did not have enough people to protect us but they damn sure wanted me to testify. I hated this shit and I was getting restless. I wonder did Tre know what was going on? I know he was trying to dig up some information but when you are in witness protection it is supposed to be hard to find the person. They wanted me to testify against Mr. Richards. His stupid ass had got caught up in some shit and he had dragged us in it too. I really don't know how they figured that I could help when Rashad and I had gotten out of the drug game a minute ago. I should have never let him talk me into this shit. I had long ago chased Italy's ass away, so Darien and Rebecca had to hire some other women to make their drug runs for them. That was why Darien was in jail in the first place and just like a true hustler he was back on it hell he was dealing in jail with the help of Italy. Elise was in Racine, Wisconsin and she was getting it popping down there and she was doing it on her own. We were trying to get people everywhere because no matter where you go there are always drug dealers and dopefiends. Mr. Richards had lost most of his businesses due to him not knowing what the hell he was doing as a businessman, but he was still in the drug game heavily. At first, I am not going to lie I was mad that Rashad wanted me to run drugs. I know he had told me a little bit of information before we got married but I never thought he wanted me to run the drugs. After being married for just three months he sprang the news on me. Rashad walked into the bedroom and smacked me on my ass. I had on some gray leggings with a baby doll white t shirt. "Damn baby why you do that?" I asked as I rubbed my ass. He really did hurt my ass. "Get dressed we gotta make a run." He said and I looked at him crazy. "I am dressed. What?" I had just put on my workout clothes and I really did not want to change. Hell, it was cold outside. "Girl please stop trying to workout I love that fat ass. But for real remember I told you to have you some attire for when we are doing business." He said and slipped off his True Religion jeans. "What? Are you for real we really about to do this?" He turned and looked at me. "For real you need to quit and get it together Niya. I told you what I was trying to do, and I thought you was a big girl since you handled that situation with your baby daddy and Bruce." He said with a stern voice. Yes, I had handled the situation with them, but my life was in danger. Selling drugs had nothing to do with my life being in danger and I knew I could go to jail. I sat on the bed "I am scared." I admitted. He sat next to me and rubbed my thigh. "Stop being scared baby you have one life to live do you want to get this money or nah?" I looked in his gray eyes and fell in love all over again. What was I scared of I knew this man, he would protect me. "We need a baby sitter."I said. He kissed me and jumped up. "I got that covered. Moms gone watch the kids Pops coming with us since technically he supposed to still be running shit." I got dressed and put on what he had told me to put on. He told me to put some joggys on so that they could be loose, and a plain tee shirt with some tennis shoes. I opted for some gray joggys, a black t shirt with my black Adidas. I put on my black long wig with the bang. Rashad did not want people to recognize me. After we conducted business with Mr. Richards the first time his father took the drugs to his house and we went home. His mother left and we fed the kids just like we had not been anywhere. I had been nervous the entire time, but it was pretty simple. We met at a restaurant where Rashad, Mr. Richards, Mr. Thompson, and I sat to have lunch. I excused myself and went to the ladies room. In the last stall there was a broken sign on the door. I went in there and there was a purse and inside the purse was the drugs. I put my purse down and took that purse. As I exited the stall a Mexican girl with long wavy hair came into the bathroom. She went into the stall that I was in and I knew that was the person who was supposed to get the money. I washed my hands and once I knew that she had the purse I went back out to talk to the boys. I looked around the restaurant and I spotted the girl ten minutes later sitting with a bunch of girls chatting it up like nothing ever happened. It was simple and after doing it that one time I was not so scared anymore so anytime, after that was a piece of cake. That was how we started off but as Mr. Richards started to become trusting of us, he let us come to his house. Of course, he was a fucking idiot and I did not like working with him. I hated the tardiness I hated how he always tried to get over on us. It was pure bullshit. I did not know why Rashad wanted to be the kingpin of the streets hell we had enough money I did not understand why he still wanted to hustle. I will admit the first years it was fun. We were making money, but the thrill went out of the ride when problems kept coming up. Rashad acted like it was okay that this was how hustling was and maybe it was. I felt like it was not the life for me, but Rashad had hustled his entire life. Mrs. Thompson used to run the streets, but he also suffered a breakdown with the situation that happened to Rebecca. A Cuban guy El came on the scene and Rashad and Darien had linked up with him. They still had ties to him up until we started dealing with Mr. Richards. Why they did not stay working with El was a mystery to me. I think it had to do with the fact that Mr. Richards was a nice guy although he fucked up a lot, he was a man who you could chat with and consider family. The one time that I met El I could tell he was a killer. He did not give a damn he was a street ass Cuban. The look in his eyes was enough to scare you. Hell, I did not even hear him speak but I could feel the danger in his vibe. We were out having dinner and we happen to run into El and Rashad stopped and spoke while El gave him a nod. I felt some type of way about it, but Rashad just ushered me to the table. El did give me a bad vibe so I could see why Rashad dealt with Mr. Richards. Three years we were dealing with Mr. Richards. It was times when our clients were ready to kill us because of all the fuckups that Mr. Richards was doing. It was not even worth it neither. We were not making a ton of money like in the beginning. It was like we were only getting paid from our companies. Rashad was angry about that shit and he was really getting pissed because he felt the kids and I was in danger. "Bae this stupid muthafucka done fucked up again." He came into the kitchen of our castle. He looked tired and his gray eyes looked a bit red. I knew he was mad because he had a cigarette in his hand and that was unusual for him. He had quit smoking before I met him but dealing with a dummy like Mr. Richards it will cause you to smoke. "What happened baby?" I asked while I threw the crab legs in the boiling water. Rashad sat at the kitchen table and smoked his cigarette. "So you know I started fucking with Luke down in Miami? Why I just got the call that the damn package was light. It's like damn I will have to start opening shit up. This not a part of my job description. Fuck! All I'm supposed to be doing is connecting with different muthafuckas from city to city, state to state and delivering the shit. Now I gotta make sure the shit is all there." "Baby you know that muthafucka be shorting a people that is why I always make sure when I am delivering shit is right. I mean look how long we been fucking with Al and look how many times he done fucked up you gotta think ahead of the game bae." He couldn't do anything but shake his head. Shit I did not know why Rashad would even deliver some shit he did not check especially since he knew how Mr. Richards was slipping. I was a runner for the drugs for a while, but after too many fuck ups and Rashad being afraid for me, he started doing the deliveries himself. Well he hired some chicks to do it. At first, we had to deal with the shorts and shit like that. I made sure to check my packages. Before I left any spot that I went to pick a package up from I counted that shit. The nigga had put my life in danger far too many times and I was not having it. If shit was short, I would tell his ass and make sure they came correct. Mr. Richards did not even like to see me coming he knew I was about business. I got tired of that shit, the thrill of it played out Rashad had Juanita and Stacey making runs for us. Juanita was a bitch who swore up and down that she was going to be a stripper. When she became a stripper then I would become a stripper she was ten pounds lighter than me and thought she was the shit. I must admit I was a bit jealous of her. She was a hot little young thing. She was a redbone just like me and I can say that her fat was in all the right places, but she had a gut just like I did. She always wore different color purple hairstyles and she swore she was fly. To be honest I did not know if it was my imagination or what, but I swore

I Rashad had a thing for the chick. "I know I have to teach them somethings. We can keep blaming Mr. Richards all I want but at the end of the day our reputation is on the line." I told Rashad. We had to get a hold of things. People were not going to be looking for Mr. Richards they would be looking for us. I gave him a kiss and reassured him that everything would be alright. Luke the guy from Miami stopped fucking with Rashad. He better been glad that when things like that happen people just stopped fucking with us because it could have ended up a lot worse. We had lost so much clientele along the way that it was ridiculous. I was tired of the drug game especially because it was causing us so many problems. Rashad had turned into an entirely different person and after a while I just wanted this shit to be over with. I know he wanted to fill his father's shoes, but he was not cut out for it. After years things just started to get worse. At first, we were making dough but after a while people did not want to fuck with us and it was making it harder for us to get clientele because of it. Mr. Thompson had been given up being a kingpin within a year of going back to the lifestyle. He settled back into being a retired husband. Some men are not cut out to be a street nigga and I could tell that the lifestyle was not for him nor Rashad too much shit was happening. I just wanted Rashad to give up the lifestyle too. Now his brother Darien he was cut out for the lifestyle. Even he had wavered off from us to do his own thing because he got tired of having to deal with the shorts and the bullshit from Mr. Richards. It would have been easier for them to just kill the old man but then they did not want the unnecessary drama. No one knew how many people were really in Mr. Richard's organization.

Chapter Eight
ANIYA

Damn I was tired of sitting in this damn house and I knew the kids were tired of it too. I was in witness protection because Mr. Richards. They say he is a dangerous man. The FEDS really did not know as much as they thought about Mr. Richards. I didn't know how many killers he had on his team, but one I knew for sure was Crenshaw, his nephew. It still brought chills up my body just thinking about Crenshaw. Crenshaw was the look alike of my baby's daddy Hakeem, but he was gangsta and it was something about that man that kept me wondering. The way he looked at me made my body scream and the way he talked to me made me cream. We played the scream, cream game for so damn long that I wanted to jump his bones every time I saw him. He didn't live in Atlanta he was from New York. He didn't have a New York accent though, so it always made me wonder where he was really from. His mother was Mr. Richard's sister and Crenshaw's father was all nigga. You could tell because Crenshaw looked nothing like a Mexican. That was okay I loved his thug style it turned me on. Had I not been married to Rashad then I would have jumped his bones in a split second. But that don't mean we have never crossed paths in a romantic way and because of that it always have, me fantasizing about what could be. It was December almost close to Christmas and I was picking up a few things from the Mall. Chick-Fil-A was my favorite spot to go to whenever I went out to the mall. We never had one in Wisconsin until recently and I had moved by then. I loved a great chicken sandwich and I went to stand in line and I spotted Crenshaw. I didn't know he was in town and he was looking good as ever with his True Religion white and baby blue outfit and some Jordans that matched. He looked good and his braids were freshly done with a fresh lining. I got in line and pretended as if I did not know him. I had a big neck sweater dress that fell just above my knee and I had on some peanut butter suede flat thigh high boots. That was one thing I loved about Atlanta they did not have snow storms, like Wisconsin so the salt and snow did not eat away at my suede boots. I had my hair in a simple short cut that I had seen on Nia Long and I was rocking it right just like I always do. I was pretending like I did not know him, but he made sure to acknowledge that he knew me. He smiled when he saw me and them gold snatch outs was glowing. I knew Crenshaw was a young thug but I for some reason was feeling him. I did not know if it was because he reminded me of Hakeem or what but he was definitely fuckable. "What up lil mama?" He walked up and stood next to me. Damn he smelt good. That little single line opened a whole different world for me. We ordered our food and we sat together, and we talked about everything. I have to say Crenshaw was a good guy and just like I thought he was younger he was twenty-seven and at the time I was thirty-three. That was when I was still caught up in the idea of Rashad's dream. Thinking about Crenshaw made me think about what he said that day. Crenshaw made a rather funny statement that I had been thinking but had never spoken out loud. "Not to be funny or anything like that. Fuck it I am trying to be funny. Don't you think your husband too old to try to get in the drug game at this age?" I rolled my eyes not in a fuck you, nigga but in a damn, I know type of eye rolling. I didn't say anything because I was not going to down talk my husband. I loved Rashad and that was not going to change just because he came up short on his pipe dream. "Well you know we all have dreams" I stated with little enthusiasm behind it. Crenshaw knew that statement was bullshit just like I did. Truth be told I really did not know why Rashad wanted to get in the drug game so heavily now that he was older. Hell, it was time to go legal all the way and he was doing it backwards. I did not understand it. We did still have the strip club and a restaurant that we owned, and we were doing well. We had those companies in Wisconsin so why Rashad wanted to be in the drug game bewildered me. I took down Crenshaw's number you know just any time I wanted to talk. That night I lay next to Rashad and I asked him the question that I dare not speak but I spoke it. We were laying, in bed after we just had made love. That was one thing Rashad had covered he was a beast in the sheets, and I believe that is what kept me coming back. Not only that but Rashad was a sweetheart to me and the kids. He loved my children as if they were his own. I still wanted to know more about his little boy, but he did not know so he could not tell me. But he did know something that I did want to know and that was about this whole drug dealer idea.

"Rashad baby don't take this the wrong way but why do you want to be a drug dealer?" I asked as I lay in his arms. He laughed so that made me feel better because I really did not want to hurt his feelings. "I love the thrill of it. Remember my father was a drug kingpin back in the days and I put in a lot of work in for him. I have done some things that I am not proud of, but I did it because I believed one day, I would run these Atlanta streets. When that shit happened with Rebecca, we were young I stepped back to make sure that my sister was okay. That made away for Darien to step up because I had stepped back. Naturally we both wanted the number one spot, but Darien proved to the streets that he was more dependable. I on the other hand kind of lost touch with the streets in those years. My father had a nervous breakdown and the streets looked at him as if he was weak. That is what fucked up our reputation. Darien had to go through hell and high water to prove to niggas that he was not a soft ass nigga. My father ain't a soft ass nigga but he was going through so much at the time that he just couldn't take it. People don't understand that especially not niggas on the streets. Niggas turned on him so swiftly that you would have thought that they had it in their minds already. We never really got back in the dope game like we should have. We did our thang a little bit, but we are not where we need to be in the game. We should be at the top of the food chain and here we are at the bottom. I just wanted to be like my father I want the power. I do want to own companies and have legit money, but I also want to make these streets fear me. That was always a goal of mine." He said as his eyes glistened in the darkness. That was some stupid shit but at the same time I felt him. He wanted what he felt like was owed to him just like I did with the businesses that Hakeem built. That was something that was owed to me and if someone tried to snatch it from up under me I was going to fight to the death of me. I proved that with Bruce. Rashad was not cut out for the drug game I don't know if he was once a killer but that side of him had died down. Now he was letting niggas get away with shit that any other nigga would have killed them for especially a nigga trying to become a kingpin. That shit Rashad said never made sense to me but who was I too judge because I was not the smartest student in the class. Here I was a thirty-six-year old millionaire and I could not even touch my money. That was some bullshit. I always kept my money separate from Rashad and I did not want anyone to find my bank accounts. I had my information still under Hakeem's name. He had our account under a joint account, and he put my name as Aniya Harris-Turner thankfully I had not changed it and I hoped like hell that they never found it. I needed that for when I broke away and started a new life. I had done so many things that this was not going to be difficult for me. I just wanted Malcolm and Deena to know that whatever we went through that Mommy had their backs and was not leaving them for nothing. I had ruined their lives in my eyes and I just wanted to give them the world. After all this was over, I just wanted to be a better mother. I kept getting myself into these fucked up situations with these men and I was tired of it.

Chapter Nine

ANIYA

The first time I laid my eyes upon Malcolm I was relieved. I wanted him here with me first because he understood more than Deena. Malcolm was just like his father he was strong. He looked just like the man too. He was only twelve, but he stood over me a couple of feet, but he was still a Mama's boy. We always had that bond since he was little. All the beatings that I took in front of him I know that he remembered. He was a child, but I know that he could still remember the fear that we both experienced because of their father. I think he knew the reason why his father was dead, but he never said anything about it. He was old enough to understand that his father beat me. I just hoped that as he got older, he did not turn into a woman beater. He seemed like a reserved young man but so did his father. I was learning that you never knew who a person was just by looking at them. When Dale brought Malcolm to me after he had taken him from Mya's house, I hugged my son so tight. He laughed. "Dang Mama calm down I am alright." His gray eyes sparkled. Ugh he looked like his father. Yes, handsome as he was, I hoped he was not going to be a heartbreaker like his father. "Shut up boy I missed you so much." I said and hugged him again. "Whatever we gone stay in this little apartment?" He asked looking around. It was little compared to what we were used to. It had a living room with a small kitchen. There were two small bedrooms and in the room, that he and Deena was going to be in it was two twin sized beds. I had a full-size bed, but it was lumpy. We did have cable but that was it. I was not supposed to have a cell phone, but I did. We were in a situation that we were not used to. "Yea it will be over soon." I said trying to uplift his spirit. "I ain't tripping Mama as long as we together" that statement brought a tear to my eye. He had told me about being at Mya's house. He loved Mya both of my kids did. She was a good person and she wore her heart on her sleeve. Malcolm said that Deena did not think that I was coming back for them. That was just like my daughter to doubt that I was coming back. He said that Deena would cry at night and snuggle next to him because she was scared, and she missed me. That made me smile because Deena never really showed that much affection towards me, I was happy to know my baby girl loved me as much as I loved her. My kids were my life and I could not believe I had put us in this damn predicament. I loved Rashad but I loved my children more. I just wanted all this bullshit to be over that way we could move on with our lives. Rashad was out of our lives and that saddened me, but it is what it is. After dealing with Hakeem and Bruce I was not for the disrespect and Rashad knew that but for some reason after we got married the muthafucka forgot but ain't nothing like a little gunfire to make a person remember. I kept making sure the kids were okay in the room, but I really wanted to get out the house. Being in a small space like that was semi driving me crazy and I did not like it. Here I was in another fucked up situation because of a man. Damn I was stupid I really needed to learn that men are not good for me. First it was Hakeem with his abusive ways, and he kept me in messed up situations because I was always trying to explain why my ass was beat. The nigga was taking care of me with my own money the way I looked at it. I had every excuse for why I could not leave him. First it was because I loved him, then it was because I was pregnant, then I was depending on him financially. I left him in another way because death is a way of leaving that you can't take back. Sometimes I regret killing Hakeem because I do have a heart but other times, I be like he deserved it. Bruce was a whole other type of asshole who tried to leave me broke and busted. I promise that beautiful devil was deceiving me from the beginning. I was too blind to see because he treated me like an equal at first something I had never experienced with Hakeem. Bruce made me feel like a woman like a smart business savvy woman. Which is I was, but he used my knowledge to his advantage. In the end he was the one who got fucked. That is one muthafucka I do not regret killing because he was sick and nasty. I should have left his brother Rashad ass in Atlanta and not married him. He was gorgeous every woman who could see would stop and look and at him. Ugh I wish I did not stop and look at him. Who was I kidding I loved that man to pieces. Sure, I had to kill him, but I still loved him. Just like I loved Hakeem and Bruce I loved Rashad. The love I had for them was not going to change the fact that they each had done me wrong in some type of way and because of that I had to kill them. Rashad's death was different though. I loved and killed Hakeem because I was scared for my kids and my life. I was tired of the abuse and I did not want him to hurt my children. Bruce's death was strictly revenge. He tried to take the companies that brought me money to support my children and I. Although I had tricked him into signing over the companies to me, he still needed to learn not to fuck with me. But Rashad's death was from pure hurt. He had hurt my feelings and broken my heart and I killed him. It was like I was a black widow the way these men were coming up dead and I was asking myself maybe it was me. Was I attracting the wrong men? Shit Hakeem had issues since he was younger, but I could see how I had attracted him because I was vulnerable at the time. I was being raped and beaten by my mother's boyfriend. That was no way to live. The dumbest thing I did was tell Hakeem my problems with James. He saw that I was a broken woman and he used that against me so that I could trust him. I fell from him instantly like a dumb ass. Bruce he was just sick all around the board and I was not even going to blame myself for that. I was vulnerable at the time I was just looking for a nice time and that was what he gave me. He had an ulterior motive that was not something I could have seen written on his forehead. Rashad, I have to admit I really did not mean to kill him.

It just happened and that is why I blocked his death out of my mind. That is why I am so scared to think about it because truth be told I do not feel like dealing with the consequences of my actions. That is why I am here now trying to save my life and my kid's life. Just like a coward I do not want to go to jail. I damn sure do not want to die so I set it up where neither one would happen, and I would disappear. Mr. Richards was taking too long and I was getting antsy. I went to my bedroom. I lay on the bed and stared at the ceiling as I thought about Crenshaw. We had become good friends and I loved his conversation. He was the opposite of Rashad he wanted to get out of the drug game and if things went right, I really wanted to help him. Here I was supposed to be mourning the death of Rashad but here I was wondering about another man. Life be like that sometimes. I was hurting I couldn't deny that, but I had been through so much that I was trying to block it out. That was my problem I killed one man and went to another with no time to think. That was my way of dealing with things whether it was wrong or right. I wanted to text Crenshaw but my conscious would not allow it. I knew what it was too. It was that voice telling me that I was wrong that I shot and killed Rashad for no reason. Damn I hated myself for that shit. He had pushed me though he had pushed me too far. He knew I had gone through shit with my baby daddy and his brother, so I did not see why he felt the need to put me through more shit. Rashad and I had a great marriage don't get me wrong things were not just all bad. Besides us running drugs together we owned the strip club and the restaurant together. The strip club which I renamed Sophisticated Sluts had really started making money. To be honest Rashad did a marvelous job running things as a boss. We always made sure that things ran smoothly at Sophisticated Sluts. We had a theme for every day of the week so that we kept money flowing seven days and it was actually Rashad's idea. Monday Madness was where the women who had beef would come and fight at the club like a real boxing match. The one who lost would not be able to perform on stage that upcoming weekend so them bitches would be fighting for their life hell they needed their money. There were these two women who kept getting into it. Diamond and Vanity always got into because they felt like each other were stealing the other person customers. I had watched and Diamond was stealing Vanity's customers. Diamond was a brown skinned big teeth chick that had an ass fat like K. Michelle. She was not a looker, but her body was one to die for. Her titties were at least a triple D and they sat up so perky and pretty that even I stared when she got naked. Vanity was all face she was gorgeous. She was a Puerto Rican cutie and she had the most gorgeous eyes that you had ever seen. When she added the right touch of makeup on those brown, gold mines she could make you fall in love by just the way she stared at you. Her body was okay, but she was not Diamond. When Monday Madness came around Vanity was ready to put a pounding on Diamond. Although she was a beauty queen, she put hands on Diamond so bad that you would have thought she was the ugly bitch. Tranny Tuesdays was always fun when we had our fellas from the gay community perform. Rashad did not like that but hey I was part owner and I loved the fellas and truth be told we made most of our money that night. Those men would throw on some padded bras, some padded shorts, get dressed and work that stage without even being naked. WildNOut Wednesday was where we had the mud wrestling matches for the chicks it was pure entertainment. We got a lot of older white men in on that night and they loved to spend money. Those white men were crazy about that mud wrestling shit. I hated it because it cost too much money and the cleanup was something serious. Throwback Thursdays was when we would do an old school theme and have the old folks come in and enjoy the music of the Temptations, Jazz, or Blues them old women would get drunk and try to get on stage and work the pole. Fridays and Saturdays were all about the strippers. Sunday was a chill day and we would show the game. Sophisticated Sluts was racking in money, so we really did not need the drug money. It was just like Rashad said he had something to prove. I loved the man that was no lie, but his way of thinking was something that I was not ready for. Hakeem was never into the streets. I remember when Chiquita seen how much money that Hakeem was making, and she accused him of selling drugs. That day you could see the fire in his eyes as he stormed into the apartment. He slammed the door behind him, and it startled me to the point that I was scared and thought that he was going to hit me. He hit me so much that everything made me flinch. Even if we were having a good day which was rarely, I still flinched. He walked up to me with fire in his eyes I had just put Deena down for her nap. After I had Deena the beatings had become so bad that I prayed right then and there that he was not going to hit me. Even Malcolm had stopped playing with his Tonka truck in anticipation of his Father's rowdy behavior. He sat down on the couch and looked at me "Do you know what the fuck Quita had the nerve to ask me?" I just stared and waited for a response he was asking a question but after years of being with him I knew that he did not want a response. "Her fat ass gone say so you making, all this money you must be a dope boy now. What kind of shit is that?" He yelled louder than a lion roared, and it shook my soul. "She stupid as hell I am smart! I can build a damn country by myself if I needed to what the fuck do she mean? Every man is not a damn drug dealer." He yelled. He was right a couple of times that I was with Chiquita she had commented about Hakeem. She would say things like that boy is a kingpin I know it, but she would have a smile on her face. After finding out about Chiquita it seemed like she wanted Hakeem to fail. She wanted him to be just another thug in the streets. I know she got pleasure out of him beating on me. Truth was that Hakeem was smart I could admit to that. He did not even go to business school he just had money that Chiquita helped him get and he started up his companies. I think she used it from her "foster parents" insurance policy. I knew that he was smart because everything that I learned in business school Hakeem was doing. If he was alive right now, he would be a multi-millionaire probably a damn billionaire, but he had fucked up. Chiquita was an evil bitch that I did not like. I wonder how she was holding up in jail. I had not heard from her, but I hope she was living in hell. Damn shame she tried to kill me. She was not right in the head and I just wished that somebody could have gotten her, Hakeem, and Vanessa some help because they were crazy as hell. Even Hakeem's other baby mama was crazy, so I wasn't surprised that they had turned me into a damn nutcase. Cedes had tried to reach out to me too. She had written me a letter that I never read. I had just recently got the letter before all this shit happened and I didn't get a chance to read it. To be honest I was not trying to read it. The mail had come to the new house because I had all my mail forwarded to my new address. Five years later and she had decided to write me. I am sure it was all a bunch of bullshit she did not want anything from me, and she really did not have anything to say to me after she had tried to frame me for murder.

Chapter Ten

ANIYA

I had stolen a phone a couple of weeks ago when I was out with Dale and I had used it to call Mr. Richards immediately. I wanted him to know that I was not going to tell on him. He reassured me that he would have someone come to get me so that I could move on and relocate. I don't know how I was a part of this bullshit when I had told Rashad a while ago that we were getting out of the drug business. Mr. Richards was being investigated and I told Rashad that it was time to stop dealing with him. He was not trying to hear me. I knew for a fact that Mr. Richard was being investigated because he was too damn suspicious. All the years that we had dealt with this man he was never on time and now all his drop offs were perfect. Hell, half the time his workers would be at the spot before us. That was not like Mr. Richards. He was a man who thought that people had to work around his schedule, so I knew that something was up. Plus, I had talked to Crenshaw and he had told me that his uncle was being investigated. Crenshaw had even stopped dealing with his uncle. I wanted to tell Rashad what Crenshaw had told me, but I couldn't explain why he even had my number. Rashad had given me a ring and told me til' death do us part I wanted the death part to be done by someone else or something else. I did not want to be the one to do the deed, but I had done it. I am not going to lie Rashad was not who I had thought he was before we had gotten married. He is a genuinely sweet guy, but he was not business smart. I could see why he had been calling his brother Bruce for his advice. Rashad was smart but he was just all over the place he was not organized. Once he got a grip on stuff it was just like he took it and scattered it around just like a child throwing coins. When we had gotten married, he had done some great things to the strip club do not get me wrong. We were making money, but the strip club was in chaos. The strippers were sleeping with the bouncers and the customers. Some of the customers were having fights over the strippers it was a pure mess. Mariah was a Puerto Rican and black chick who looked fully African American if you asked me. She was cute enough with a fat ass and slim waist. Apparently, she was sleeping with the bouncer Derek. He was a tall caramel colored lanky nigga that looked like if you hit him, he would just fall over. I don't know if that was true because Derek would hit a nigga one time and he would be out cold. I guess he had to be swift on his feet since he was so skinny. Mariah and Derek were fucking around, and Mariah was also fucking with a customer. I don't know who the nigga was, but he was ugly. He was brown skinned, about 5' 2, way too short for her 5'7 height. He had black spots on his face, and he had short braids that barely touched his neck. He would come in from time to time and somewhere along the line Mariah and him, had started fucking. One Friday, there was not a lot of customers in the club just yet. It must have been something going on because we always kept customers in our place. I was at the bar talking to Trickzy the bartender. I liked Trickzy because she was straight up and kept everything real. She was a short brown skinned diva with pink hair. We were sipping on a beer talking shit about how dead it was in the place. A white stripper by the name of Bunny was still on the stage shaking her ass just for fun because it was only about three men in there. All the other ladies were in the back and Mariah was in the back sitting on Derek's lap. It was unprofessional but Rashad had let these people get too comfortable with him that they thought they could do anything. Beyonce 'The Best Thing I Never Had' was playing in the background so you know that we were on bullshit because that is not a song to be played in a stripclub. Dj Shell she must have been down but that was no reason to have us in our feelings and as bad as I wanted her to turn it off it was sounding good and I was in my feelings thinking about Hakeem. I didn't even notice the little ugly guy that Mariah was fucking on come in the club with about fifteen niggas. Trickzy had to get me out of my zone and I had to get back on the job. Dj Shell was back on it and started playing Juvenile "Back That Ass Up" that allowed the ladies in the back know that there were customers. I had not even paid attention to Mariah and Derek still in the corner hugged up hell they were supposed to be on their job. I did not notice them, but the ugly short guy noticed them and all I saw was the short guy getting knocked out. All his guys rushed Derek and our other three security guards had to put a stop to the rampage. They were knocking niggas out left and right and Rashad came from the back with one of the strippers Pepper. He may not have thought that I had seen it, but I did. Pepper was about eighteen, young and ripe. Her purple contacts set the look for her and she did look exotic with her light skin and platinum blonde hair. She had a different look to her that no other chick had in the club. Although she was not that blessed in the breast and butt area her look along brought her a lot of money. I knew she had a thing for Rashad not only because he was gorgeous but because he was the boss man. Pepper could smell a nigga with money, and I knew damn well that they were not just talking in that office. I called the police and they arrived, and we closed down for the rest of the night. The next day I called for a meeting and whoever did not show up was done. I was not going to negotiate nothing to talk about they were fired. When I put my foot down then that was it. I was stressed to because I felt like the bitch Pepper was getting close to my husband. The only person I had excused from the meeting was Esha because she had a sick child that she did look after during the day. We had Bunny, Pepper, Esha, Mariah, and Sandy at the time. We went through strippers more than a lady on her period uses pads. It was ridiculous. That night I fired Mariah and Derek. I really wanted to fire Pepper, but I had no reason. I explained that the horseplay was over. I stared at Rashad and dared him to say anything.

He knew I was talking about him and Pepper ass too. He had never cheated on me from my knowledge, but I had my suspicions. He was playing he wanted so badly to be on the drug scene that he was forgetting the most important thing our business together. I did not know what was wrong with him, but he was going to get a cursing too just like the rest of them. He had not come home the night before after the situation at the club. Well he came home but it was seven in the damn morning. He kept making up excuses that he had to get the club together. We were on our way home after the meeting that I had called when I started on the conversation about Pepper being in his office. "Are you fucking her?" I asked I was done playing games I had noticed that she was in his office three times and I was tired of playing stupid. Shit the bitch would give me the eye like yeah, I am fucking your man. You know that damn look that ole girl Pandora at the job was giving Yvette the evil eye after Jody wouldn't let her fuck on "Baby Boy" but I knew better I knew Rashad gave up the dick. "Who you talking about?" He asked sounding annoyed. The nerve of him. I was annoyed and mad that bastard knew who the fuck I was talking about, but he wanted to play dumb. "Pepper are you fucking her?" I asked again with my arms folded across my chest. "Stop asking me stupid shit Niya you know I am not fucking that little girl." "Yeah well why she always in your office alone with you!" I yelled I was not about to be nice about somebody cheating on me. Hakeem had cheated on me and I beat the bitch ass and left him but came back. Bruce was cheating on me but I only caught him once at the club and shit I had cheated on him before that with his brother. I really wanted to be with his brother, so I wasn't fucked up about it. But Rashad he was my husband and I loved him, and I trusted him so if he was cheating there would be consequences. "Who you getting loud with woman? I told you I ain't sleeping with that lil ass girl so shut up about it!" He boomed back. I felt a bit threatened by the way he had come at me, so I sat back in my seat, but I was still mad. I was not scared at what Rashad would do to me, but I was more afraid of what I might do to him, so I dropped it. Shit comes out of an ass and this asshole was full of bullshit. When we made it to the house, he dropped me off and sped off. I called him all night long and he kept sending me to voicemail. I wanted to know where he was, but he would not answer. I was so upset that I did not know what to do. I cried the entire night. Five that morning he came in the room where I lay and made love to me. He was drunk and he kept apologizing to me the entire morning as we made love. I never said anything I knew he was apologizing because he had cheated on me. I did not say anything either when the next night Pepper did not show up to work. He had fired her to make me feel comfortable for the time being. As soon as another young beautiful chick walked through the door, he would be on her. Pepper was the first, but she was not the last. I always had my suspicions that he was still fucking the young girl too. The rumor is that she went to work at another strip club. I went to all the strip clubs in Atlanta and I did not see her ass there. Yes, I wanted to see her and confront her, but I never saw her. I had been going to clubs for about three months before I finally gave up that girl wasn't a stripper no more and why should she be when she was being taken care of by my husband and the cold part about is I could not prove it. I felt like Rashad was cheating on me, but I couldn't prove it. So, the little friendship that I had with Crenshaw I made sure to keep it to myself. I loved the man and I was not ready to be done with our relationship. That day though, huh that day I let my emotions get the best of me and now it was truly over.

Chapter Eleven
ANIYA

ale came at ten o'clock like clockwork. He had brought some groceries all the groceries I had asked him to bring. He brought us Monopoly to play so I decided to fix some steak, potatoes, and corn with some rolls for dinner while I showed my kids how to play Monopoly. I had two hotels and one house on my property. I wasn't winning though Malcolm was killing me and Deena. He was smart he could build a country just like his father. The boy was smart and very observant. He was well mannered and did anything that I asked of him. He had grown fond of Rashad and Rashad definitely loved my kids. Deena was his little princess and he treated her as

such. Deena was a girly girl and I loved that about her.
One thing about A'Deena was she loved her big brother
and she listened very well to him. Malcolm and I were
closer than A'Deena and I. She kind of distanced herself
from me but she loved Rashad. She was a girl and she
clung on to men and their every word I could tell she was
like me she trusted men just like I did. That was not a bad
thing but sometimes it was not a good thing neither her
pretty brown eyes sparkled, every time she saw Rashad
and Malcolm. She would say "stepdaddy Mommy doesn't
want to give me any candy could you give me some?" I
would laugh my ass off, and Rashad would never give in.
He would tell her well sweetie what your mother says go
she controls me too and we would all laugh. I loved his
humor, I loved his smell, I missed him. I got up from the
kitchen table and took a break from the game. Malcolm
understood that I was going through things, but Deena
was too young she did not understand all the things that
were happening. She wanted to know when we were going
back to our castle. She wanted to know where her
stepfather was, and I did not have the heart to tell her that
he was dead. I had told Malcolm when he was brought to
me and he cried. He did not understand why all the men
in his life were taken from him. I did not have the heart to

tell him it was because of me. Every time I killed, I felt I had reason to I never stopped and thought the impact it had on my children. Yes, I knew that Hakeem would have beaten on them. Well maybe not Deena but I knew he was going to start beating on Malcolm. But would it have been better if I had just left? No! I needed to stop asking myself that because the truth is Hakeem would have been harassing us until the end. He would have showed up at my house and beat my ass and Malcolm. Things are better this way with him dead. I did what I had to do and one day when I told Malcolm and explained it to him, he would understand. I could tell my son was going to be something great and I would see to it. Whatever he wanted to be I was going to see to it that he was going to be the best him and Deena. I checked my phone and was surprised to see a text I did not want to answer it. The only person who was supposed to even know this number was Mr. Richards. After I killed Rashad, I ran out the house and the police traced me to a hotel where they put me under arrest. I had shot him and went to get the kids and went to a hotel. I told the kids that I needed a vacation, but the truth was I did a piss poor job of hiding. I was ready for them to take me in and I did not give a damn. Once I shot Rashad, I was over everything. The only reason I went to the hotel was because I wanted to spend a little time with my children before I went to jail for life. It was a nice sunny day in Georgia as usual and I was out and about and decided to take a trip to the club. Rashad had left earlier that day and I felt that he was being suspicious. I had told him that I had a lot of running around to do but I would catch up with him at the club later. That is what I wanted him to think so that I could catch his ass up. I had on my white tight leggings with a gray shirt that complimented me well. My hair was pulled into a long ponytail with a part down the middle. I was feeling good and I wanted to see my man yeah right, I wanted to see what my man was up to and if need be, I was going to whoop ass. I pulled up to the club and saw the cleaning crew was still there. We had hired a local cleaning crew which I felt was stupid since I had a cleaning crew in Wisconsin and Chicago. I opened the door and walked across the room. There was no one in there and I felt like that was unusual. I did not even see the cleaning crew. They may have gone to lunch. It was a couple of restaurants in walking distance. Usually there are about three or four people in the club cat least just kicking it and there was no one. I had to the club to see if he was fucking with a bitch, but not seeing anyone around made me fear for his life. There was a new stripper Bubbles and I felt like he was fucking on her. She was a bad ass redbone with the most hypnotizing green eyes. I think they were contacts, but they fit her so well. I had seen Rashad staring at her a couple of times and I grew suspicious. I had never caught him with anyone but that did not mean he was not doing shit all that meant was he was covering his tracks. That was my motive for coming to the club, but those thoughts faded when I thought he was in danger. Recently he had told Mr. Richards that he was done dealing with him because honestly the hustle was not getting Rashad anywhere. It was like we were nickel and diming and we were supposed to be on top. Not only that but we were getting into it with too many hustlers because of Mr. Richard's fuck ups I was scared. I had given Rashad an ultimatum that he was either going to leave the drug bullshit alone or I was leaving him. I had gotten ran off the road and I was a nervous wreck. Coming from the grocery store I got in my car and I did not notice a black SUV following me. By the time I did it was too late they rammed into my car. Years ago, I had traded in my Porsche for a red Mercedes Benz . I could not believe someone would ram into my car. I lost control of the car instantly and ran into a pole. I was okay but my car was a total wreck. That day I had seen him preparing for another drop-off. I could not believe that even after I had gotten ran off the road, he thought shit was okay. Our lives were in danger and he could not see it. When he came and got me from the hospital all he could say was baby you need to be careful. I had told his ass what happen, and he knew what was up, but he wanted to act like the shit was nothing. I could not take it any longer I snapped. He was sitting in the living room and he hung up the phone. I walked over to him. "Who was you talking to?" I asked. "The girls we got another drop off" he said like a true boss. After years we were not getting any money really because we had tried to keep our transactions to a minimum. That is how Rashad wanted it he wanted to make sure we did work but not too much it was not making any sense to me. Hell, we were not making a big profit and the time and energy we were using making "drop offs" we could have been doing that building another company. "What the fuck Rashad we not making no money and the drop-offs are unnecessary." I said and sat down next to him. "What you trying to say Niya because I'm not getting what you trying to say?" I could tell he was irritated with me and he really wanted to slap me, but he knew better. "I said it clear

Rashad don't take this the wrong way but baby the drug thing is just not popping for us. Hell, we were making more money in the beginning. Five years later we only making five hundred dollars you know that is chump change." He did a long sigh as he put his hand over his face. I knew that meant he agreed with me. "I know baby, but I just wanted to make it big," he said as he kicked the table. Defeat was written all over his face. He wanted to be like his father and be a kingpin, but his time had passed. He needed to let it all go. "Fuck the drug game let's take over the strip club industry or the food industry try something new and different babe." He grabbed me and gave me a long kiss. "That's why I love you because you so damn smart. You right I am too old for this shit my time has passed." He told me he was going to get out of the drug game, but we had fucked over so many people and came up short so many times that I assumed that someone was after him too. I loved that man and I knew that he loved me so when I opened the door to his office at Sophisticated Sluts, I damn near lost my mind. The muthafucka wasn't in danger nope not yet. Nothing could have prepared me for the shit I had seen. My body was sweating, and I could feel my trigger finger itching. I had been going to the gun range and I can brag that I had gotten pretty good. I was pissed at what was in front of me, but I was sad too. The blood boiling within my body had risen to the top but it also had started steam and the steam had turned into tears. I felt the tears falling from my eyes as Rashad looked up from the chair as he was getting head.

Chapter Twelve
ANIYA

His gray eyes were in shock as he tried to tap the girl's head and make her stop. She was going to town on his dick as her head bobbed up and down. It felt like a lifetime had passed before she had finally stopped. I was mad but most importantly I was hurt. "What big daddy I heard her mumble?" The nerve of that bitch to be calling my husband big daddy she was out of her mind. "Get up damnit!" He said in a stern voice. I would have been ran up on her but I wanted to see who the fuck this bitch was. He pointed in my direction and when I saw that it was Trickzy. Her eyes widened, but it was too late as I pushed her up against the wall. "No Niya I am sorry," she said as I beat on her face. I was throwing punches left and right and I could feel Rashad trying to grab me off her. I turned and gave him a punch that Ali would have been proud of and turned around and continued to beat her face. This was the first time that Rashad seen me in action, and I knew it surprised him that I could move so fast and my punches were so hard. She was trying to block the blows, but I was beating her through the blocks. I jumped up and was blood was everywhere. My white leggings had red blood streaks on them, and my gray Adidas did too. You would have thought I just did a massacre with all the blood on me. I stormed out the club and jumped in my car. I was getting my shit and getting the fuck out of there. There meaning the house that we built together. I could not believe Rashad could be so selfish. Yes, I had my suspicions but what bitch don't. If your man is making money and look as good as Rashad, you would be thinking that he would be creeping too. All the late nights and shit hell I had my reasons to think he was cheating. All my suspicions and questioning wasn't shit to actually seeing it with my own two eyes. My heart was broken into a million pieces. To be honest I do not even know how I made it home. The tears were flowing heavily, and my brain was going to come out of my head. I could not believe this muthafucka had the nerve to be cheating on me and with Trickzy. Trickzy was a chick that I had hired as a bartender for the club. Trickzy was a chick that I liked and was a person that I trusted. Everyone that I had trusted turned on me and it was too much. From my Mama, to Hakeem, to Bruce, to Chiquita, to Cedes, to Rashad I stopped for a second and screamed out. "Who can I fucking trust! Ugh!" I raced inside the big castle that I called a home and ran through my living room. It smelled of bacon still from the breakfast I had cooked. I ran up the stairs to the end of the hall that was my room, our room. I had never loved someone as much as I loved Rashad, he made me smile from the beings of my soul. He gave me complete control whatever I did not want then he did not want. He was my best friend I could talk to him about anything I trusted him, and he had broken that trust for a sloppy ass blowjob. I needed to get out of that house. I guess Rashad was behind me when I was driving because it was not even five minutes later, and he was in the room with me. I was throwing his clothes around. I had come to a realization that I was not about to get out, but Rashad definitely had to go. I was not the one who broke our vows for a cheap thrill. I was not the one who stayed lying and stayed messing with unnecessary bitches. He was and he had me fucked up. I started throwing his suits away. The ones I bought so that he could look more professional. They went first because he wasn't shit but a common thug so why waste, my time trying to make him into a gentlemen. A fucking waste of my time trying to help him become business savvy he wasn't! I had gotten to the hats that he loved so much but he had made it to the house by then. My body was a sweaty mess. My once neat ponytail was disheveled and there was still blood that covered my body. I did not know if Trickzy was okay or not and to be honest I did not give a damn. Fuck that cheap hoe. I felt sorry for the bum bitch and gave her job, and this is how she repaid me by fucking my husband. She came into the club with a sad ass story that she just moved from Texas and she needed a job bad. She said that her Auntie would keep her kids at night for her for them couple of hours, but she needed to start right away. I liked her she seemed genuine, but that hoe, wasn't shit just like the rest of them. I should have kicked her ass back to Texas since she wanted to be a fucking hoe. My thoughts at first was to leave and never return but I had paid for this house and was still paying for this house, so the kids and I was going to stay Rashad had to go. He rushed me when he saw that I was throwing his hats. "Stop girl what you doing?" I turned around and smacked him so hard his cheeks turned red. We stared each other down as if he was one of my children that were contemplating whether he wanted to hit his mother. He chose the ladder just like a child and decided against it because I was ready to go to war on his ass. He did not know that I was a fucking beast and I may not be able to beat his ass, but I was damn sure going to put up a fight. He saw the damage that I did to Trickzy and if I gained on him just right, I would fuck him up too. I saw that he was not going to do anything, so I politely turned around and started throwing his shit some more. "Calm down Niya you need to just chill! Why is you throwing my stuff!" He sounded like a whiny baby as he picked up his hats. "Fuck you bitch ass nigga! Get all of your shit." I screamed so loud that I did not even recognize my own voice. He looked startled as I talked to him, but I was not through. "All you want to do is cheat with these whores they can have your ass muthafucka I am done but you you gots to go." I said as I started to throw his clothes from the drawer. He came up behind me and wrapped his arms around me. "Calm down please" he said in a calming tone. I was too angry, and I was not falling for that shit. He had his arms around me and had guided me to the bed and sat me on his lap. "Can we talk like adults please?" He asked. I agreed. The only reason being I was tired, and I needed to catch my breath. My chest was heaving up and down. "Look I don't know what you think Niya but at this point I need to be straight with you. I am seeing Trickzy." I didn't even say anything I just looked at him like he was crazy. "We have been dating for a while now and I just wanted you to know that." Before I knew it was rolling over in laughter this had to be a joke. Did he just say they were dating for a while? Wow a married man dating he had lost his mind. Once I got myself together, I stood up and looked at Rashad. "So, what are you trying to say?" I asked I did not get what he was saying but I did get what he was saying, and I did not like it. "What I am saying is that you are my wife and Trickzy is my girlfriend. I am not leaving you and I am not leaving her. You will share me when I have free time, but we are not breaking up. I am not breaking up with Trickzy and you and I are not getting a divorce" He said, and it was unreal that all I could do was walk away. I walked to the bathroom and I was in tears. I cried on the seat of the edge of the tub. I had locked the door and Rashad was out there banging on the door. I think that he was screaming for me to open the door, but it all sounded like gibberish and bullshit to me. I could not believe that a man that I had given my heart to once again had let me down. He had said that shit so calm and cool that I just knew I was dreaming. Everyone in my life had let me down. From the day that I was born my father had left. He didn't even know what I was going through and he left me with that insane woman who I called a Mother. She wasn't shit and she made my life worse than it had to be. Then I met Hakeem who was supposed to help me from that sick ass James and yes, he did but he tricked me so that he could abuse me. All the money in the world was not going to hide the fact that I had been battered, abused, and mistreated. Not just by one person but by so many. The tears kept falling I could not take it. I was shaking so hard as I cried my eyes out. I befriended Cedes because I felt like she was someone that I could have in my life and the bitch had set me up to go to jail for murder. Chiquita, I had let into my life because of Hakeem. I knew that I should have left her alone, but I wanted somebody in my corner I needed somebody in my corner, and I thought it would be her. That bitch was trying to kill me, and she was probably trying to kill my kids. It truly did hurt that I could not trust anybody. All the money in the world could not change the fact that I was lonely. Yes, I had my kids but I needed companionship, I needed friendship. It seemed like the only person I could trust was Mya. My dear friend Mya and I had been lying and keeping secrets. Poor girl was so worried about me and my trifling ass couldn't even return her phone calls when she was the one who was keeping my business coming in with revenue. Poor girl had been nothing but a friend to me and I could not even send a damn email saying hey, best friend. Shame on me I was sitting here chasing this no good muthafucka while he was chasing these young hoes like their pussy was made of gold. I was so focused on Rashad that I had lost sight of myself. Hell, I did not really know myself because I was in and out of relationships so much that I had got lost with being with men who only wanted to fuck me over. I had no identity who was Aniya Turner well Aniya Thompson I laughed. I pulled myself up and looked in the mirror. My face was dirty, and tear streaked. I looked like I was crazy, and I knew for certain I had lost my mind. I felt dirty so I ran me some bath water. I loved the white on white bathtub that we had it always made me feel clean. As I stepped into the hot water, I could hear Rashad picking up his clothes singing. "Boyfriend number two cause the first one he don't, really seem like he know what to doooo." That was muthafucka was off key. "And I know you like it freaky, so I'm gone give it to yooouuu!" I could picture his ass dancing around the room feeling like he had won. "We don't fuss don't fight don't argue." That muthafucka was taunting me. I could not take it anymore. "Shut the fuck up! You scum of the fucking Earth!" I yelled so loud that I swore the window and mirrors in the bathroom shook. He stopped and I could hear him come to the bathroom door. "Damn you still mad?" He asked like that was a surprised. Rashad thought I was a joke and that sent rage through my body. He thought that I was playing with him. He knew my history and he knew that I was not to be fucked with. Aniya looked innocent and sweet on the outside, but I could murder in a heartbeat he knew that. Yes, I had only murdered two people and that meant that I could do it again. Rashad had beat up a couple of people and shot up some muthafuckas, but I did not think that he had the heart to kill. That is what he lacked on the streets. All them niggas short-changing him, and they were still walking around. If they were dead, it was because another muthafucka had did the work. Rashad did not have the heart to put in work and I did not have the heart to tell him that he lacked the ability to kill. I knew why him, and his father was not shit on these streets it was because everyone knew they would not hurt a fly. I thought he had it in him, but he didn't. One night we had to go ride out on Roger. Roger was a young cat who kept coming up short every time we came to pick up our money. He would say I will pay y'all back. It was so many muthafuckas doing that that I told Rashad that he had to make an example out of somebody, and it happened to be Roger. Terrel his cousin came with us for the ride. At first Rashad did not want me to come but I quickly reminded him of the deeds that I had done. He finally agreed to let me come. We knew where Roger was at because he thought that he was getting a delivery little did he know that we never called Mr. Richards. We met him at our usual spot one of his trap houses that had about three of his soldiers. No lie Roger was popping, and he was making dough and the reason why he was shorting us was because he knew that he could. We all had on black so that we could blend in with the night. Roger was stupid because he should have known something was up, but he didn't as soon as we came in the house. Terrel knocked Roger over with the butt of his gun and Roger fell on the floor. Before his three soldiers could react, who were all sitting on the couch playing a game Rashad and I had our guns pointed at them. They had been caught slipping they had gotten to comfortable. Rashad and I tied the boys up and he walked over to Roger and beat his face in. After about five minutes of beating him up Rashad finally spoke. He did a good job beating him up and he was bruised and bloody. "Nigga you keep coming up short on my money and I do not like that!" He yelled. It was all theatrical and no one was really scared. Hell, I was not scared we had been dealing for three years and plenty of muthafuckas came up short and all them were still walking around. If they wasn't it was because they started dealing with someone else who did not play that shit but the streets talked and they were all talking about how Rashad did not do shit. "I am done fucking with you." He got up and grabbed the suitcase full of money and was about to head out when Terrel stopped him. "What the fuck you doing cuz?" Terrel asked. He was looking pissed and so was I. Was Rashad really that green to the game? Hell, I had never sold drugs or been in illegal activity before I met Rashad, but I knew that you were supposed to put down the murder game. "Shit I am about to go nigga I got my money." Rashad said as he eased towards the door. I still had my gun on the three guys. Rashad was acting dumb all this shit for a nigga to come back on us. I had kids and at that moment I told myself if he didn't kill them I would have too. "No nigga you gotta kill these niggas or they coming back to kill you, your wife, and your kids." Terrel said. Even I knew that, and I was never one to dabble in the street life. "No, they not I spared they life we good." Rashad said and I damn near broke out into laughter this nigga was serious. Terrel knew what I knew and felt like I felt. He turned around and shot Roger in his head. Rashad screamed no but he kept right on and killed the three guys. I ran with them to the car.

Chapter Thirteen
ANIYA

⟿⟫⟐⟐⟐⟐⟪⟿

That was the stupid shit that Rashad would do so I knew he was not about that life. Terrel cursed him out the entire ride to drop him off. He kept telling him how stupid he was to bring him along knowing that he wasn't ready to bust those guns. He was telling him that he needed to be a gangsta and stop thinking that niggas on the street was just going to let shit slide. Terrel was right Rashad was too soft hearted and he thought that he was going to make it to the top of the game being a damn saint he was sadly mistaken. Rashad could have easily beat the shit out of Terrel, but he didn't. He sat there and let his cousin treat him like a punk and that was why he could not be a kingpin. I got out of the tub and patted myself dry. I smelled good and it felt like I had washed all my problems away, but I knew they were still there. I opened the door the bathroom and looked inside our room. He had sat his things neatly back in the closet. I decided to throw on some sweatpants with a black t shirt. I put on my tennis shoes and looked in the closet for my gun. He knew I had a pistol and it was loaded too. I was tired of playing with this nigga. I put the gun behind my back and went to the stairs. "Rashad!" I yelled. "Yeah I am in the kitchen!" He yelled back sounding like he was eating on something. The nerve of this muthafucka to be eating while I was upstairs hurting. He was acting like he had told me some simple shit that I was supposed to be okay with. His stupid ass was about to die, and he did not even know it. I was calm as I went down the stairs and made my way into the kitchen. Rashad was standing by the counter eating fruits and he looked up and saw me. "You still mad?" He simply asked. "Rashad are you telling me that you are not going to leave?" I asked in a calm tone. "Niya don't ask me shit" he said with an attitude "you on some dumb shit right now I told you what it was so quit being mad." I looked at him with so much hate and disgust that I almost threw up. He was looking me dead in eyes with no remorse. Maybe if I had seen that he loved me and wanted to apologize but no those gray eyes were cold. This man that I had once loved that had once loved me turned into another man right before my eyes. Why had I not seen this coming? Where was he hiding? I did not have the answer to the questions, and I was not going to ask Rashad shit. I took the gun from the back of me and undid the safety before he even knew what was going on. I shot in the chest and he fell to the ground on impact. I watched as he looked on in surprise. "Niya baby what are you doing?" I could see that the coldness in his gray eyes had turned into him being scared. It did not feel so good when the tables were turned. It did not feel so good when the person that you give your all too turns into someone else. I had always been this person underneath it all and he had gotten a glimpse of it, but Rashad had not warned me before we got married. If he had given me that option like hey babe, I am a male whore so if we get married don't think you are going to be the only one. Shit if he had given me that chance to walk away or stay then I wouldn't have to do this. I said nothing as I raised the gun again and I shot him two more times to finish him off. I went and grabbed my keys off the table. I knew the police were going to come looking for me, but they were not going to find me here. I packed a few things to take with me to the hotel. I knew that they were going to find me, but I wanted to spend time with my kids. I picked them up from camp and Malcolm could tell that something was wrong with me. He kept asking why was we going to the hotel? He was getting on my damn nerves asking all these questions like he was my daddy. "You know what Malcolm just shut the hell up I don't feel like explaining shit." I snapped at him from the front seat of my car. I looked over at him and I felt bad. I never really scolded my children, so I think that it surprised him. "I am sorry Malcolm honey I just wanna get away." I looked at him and he still looked annoyed. My poor kids I had put them through so much and here I was leaving them alone. It was only two days before the police tracked me down at the hotel. I really did not cover my track I had never had to hide out before, so the thoughts never crossed my mind to use another name. I used cash so I thought that was enough but apparently it was not. I was new to this and you could tell because two days later there was a knock at the door, and I was being handcuffed in front of my children. Deena was crying and screaming, and Malcolm was ready to fight. I told them to calm down and placed my hands behind my back. When I was able to call, I called Mya to come get my kids from the police station. They would not let her see me but that was okay I was happy that my kids were safe. They never told me that I was arrested for the murder of Rashad. Once they got me in the interrogation room, I found out that I was not arrested for murder, but they wanted me as a witness. They never ever said anything about Rashad being dead or anything. They had never said anything about finding his body and to this day I was baffled as to why they kept asking me where my husband was. Detective Noble was a white, tall, brown haired man. He was in his late thirties, but he was still a good-looking man. He had the most piercing brown eyes that could read into anybody. He started off by asking me where was Rashad? I looked at him confused I did not understand if they had not arrested for murder then what was I doing here. I thought for sure they knew that he was dead. Truth be told I could not tell him where he was either shit to my understanding, he was dead and I definitely was not going to tell them that. "The last time I saw him he was at home" and that was the truth. His partner Detective Smith who was a short red hair white woman was getting pissed and you could tell. "Bitch stop playing with us we know that you have been doing work with Mr. Richards and you were trying to run because you knew that we were coming down on your little operation." I looked at them like they were crazy.

Rashad and I had stopped dealing with Mr. Richards well I know I had. That sneaky son of a bitch I thought Rashad had still been dealing with Mr. Richards after I told him that was a waste of time. I could not believe it I was glad he was dead. Sneaky ass fucking them tramps at the club and steady dealing behind my back. He was so fucking stupid and a waste of my time. I thought that having a husband would be so much simpler, but I was wrong like so many things in my life I was wrong. Rashad was a distraction from what I should have been doing in my life and that was raising my kids and taking care of me. Just like before I let another stupid asshole in my world, and he turned it upside down. "I really do not know where Rashad is at. As far as I am concerned, I stopped dealing with Mr. Richards and my husband was supposed to too." I said matter of factly. They broke everything down to me. They said that they had been building a case against Mr. Richards since before we bought the strip club from him. They knew about us buying the club. Mr. Richards had been trying to sell off his businesses to disappear. He did disappear after we bought the club, but he came back a month later and thought that everything was okay. He started going back into his same routine. The detectives said that Mr. Richards was shorting us so much because he was getting high and that is how he started slipping. Mr. Richards connect was out in Mexico where his mother was from. He had met his cousin Miguel once and they stayed in contact because they had something in common, dope. They said that they really wanted Miguel, but he was in Mexico and he was smart unlike his cousin. They settled for Al because he had been in the drug game for a long time and they had built up so many charges on him that they did not want to lose this. Although he was a junkie himself, he was flooding the city with drugs and although he was not head huncho that was as close to him as they were going to get. They told me that if I testify that they would relocate the kids and I. I agreed hell I knew that I had killed Rashad and as soon as they had found his body that they would come looking for me and I would use this as a cop out. They kept asking me if I knew where he was, and I kept telling them no. It baffled me that the cops had not said anything about Rashad. I tried to call Rebecca with the phone I stole. I stole some minutes to go with it and activated it once I got alone. I had tried to call Rebecca, but Mya had answered. I did not know why they were at Rebecca's house. I really wanted to see what she knew and if they had any idea that I had killed Rashad. I never reached anyone. I called Mr. Richards and I told him that the police were holding me. I was not thinking at the time I told him that if he paid me then I would not say anything, but he had to come get me. He had agreed and I told him my address. That had been weeks ago because I told him that I was waiting for my kids to get with me. I just wanted out of this deal so bad. I was not thinking but if the cops did not know that I killed Rashad then I was not going to go through with this. I had no beef with Mr. Richards, but I did need more money. I needed something out of the deal.

Chapter Fourteen
MYA

I kept looking at my phone hoping that Niya would call. I would check the mailbox repeatedly just to see if she was going to send a letter. I missed my best friends and I missed my god kids. I prayed that they were okay and that everything was good. I did not understand why she had killed Rashad. Tre said that the police was not aware of any bodies found at the residence. He had called in some favors and they said that they did not find Rashad's body. There was no evidence of foul play or anything. I wanted to know what had happened and why she had stopped contacting me I worried about her so much. Tre was trying his hardest to find out some information, but he kept coming to a dead end. Tre had been a private investigator for ten years. He had started his own P.I. firm when he got out of college and he had succeeded and tracking down all types of criminal by himself. It pained him not to be able to find my best friend. He had done so much for her in the past and they had developed a bond. It was like after Niya and Rashad got married everything changed. It was like she turned to a different person. I know she was busy raising two children, having a new husband, and being a businesswoman but I felt neglected. I felt like maybe it was me because she had never really tried to be close to me. She had invited Tre and I on their honeymoon where we went to Jamaica. We had the most amazing time and to be honest this was the first trip we had ever been on. I think she asked mostly because of all the things that Tre had done for her. They paid for everything and we were so grateful. The first two days it rained something horrible. I was a bit scared but after those two days we enjoyed ourselves. The Royal Caribbean resort was gorgeous. I had never seen water so blue that you did not know where the ocean began, and the sky ended. After it had stopped raining and the sun came out Niya and I decided to enjoy ourselves at the spa. Facials and body wraps, I was used to this but Niya had never experienced anything like it. She kept looking at the ladies at the spa. "This facial stuff better not break out my face because this is all natural." We all started laughing and they ensured her that she would be fine. We enjoyed the massages of the gorgeous men of the island who talked in their native language that we did not understand. I knew they were talking about how fine us yellow women were. I could tell just by the way they were looking at us. After we pampered ourselves, we enjoyed ourselves by the pool until we were joined by our men. We did not know where they had gone and to be honest, I did not care. I was enjoying myself and I was overjoyed that she had invited us. She was paying too, and we were enjoying each other company. I never knew Niya could be so funny and I never saw her smile so beautiful. Over the years she always had a gloomy look in her eyes I never saw so much happiness in her eyes than when we were in Jamaica. That is why I could not understand why she would kill Rashad it made no sense. Tre came in that night earlier than usual at about nine. I had finished going over everything with the companies. I did not know what was going on with Niya's case because we could not get any information. I continued to deposit her share into her account. I had called Susan to check into her other companies in Chicago and she said that Rebecca had sold the company and had given Niya her share months ago. I did not understand Niya never told me any of this. The strip club that they owned was under investigation from what Tre was telling me because the guy they bought it from was under investigation for sex trafficking. Their other company was a restaurant and the manager there had contacted me after she could not get a hold of Aniya. I had to get that company back together, so Tre and I were planning a trip to Atlanta to see what was what. Tre also wanted to stop at the house to see if he could find any clues. I kissed Tre on his cheek and gave him a long hug. I loved this man and I knew he would do anything for me. Lately he had been working on case after case plus he was trying to see what was going on with my best friend. He rubbed my back and welcomed the hug. "I love you too girl" he laughed. He pulled away. "What did you cook?" He asked as he headed to the kitchen. "Nothing I have been busy I ordered some pizza though you want me to warm you up a piece?" I asked as he sat at the kitchen table. "Yeah babe that would be helpful you had a busy day?" he asked as I pulled the box of pizza out of the oven. It was still hot because I had just ordered it an hour before he had arrived. "Yes, bae it was but I am okay now that I have my sexy man here to rub my feet." I laughed and handed him his plate. He noticed that

I did not heat it up. "You just ordered this pizza didn't you?" I did a nod and he smiled. I know he do not like warmed up pizza. Once I realized what time it was I decided to order pizza. I had texted him to make sure he would be at home at the time he said he would. He gave me the time and I made sure to have my man some hot food. "You are the best. I think we should get married." He said out of nowhere "We are getting married Tre what are you talking about?" I asked. He chewed up his slice of pepperoni pizza. He like it with everything on it olives, onions, mushrooms, pepperoni, and bacon "I know honey but I am tired of waiting I want to do it now." "But we going to Atlanta to see about Aniya" I said. "Fuck that bae we can do that after we get married. I want us to go now. She will be okay and there ain't nothing we can do about her situation. She haven't told you anything and this shit is getting to me. I want to marry you and now that I have the money, I want to do it now." I thought about what he said. I wanted my best friend at my wedding. I had missed Niya so much and she did not even know it. I wanted a big wedding with my friends and family. This would be my first and hopefully my only wedding. "Where are we going to get married?" "Let's go to Vegas." He said. "But Tre I want my first wedding to be big and I want my best friend by my side." I truthfully told him. "Come on Mya we have waited long enough. I have the money. To be honest instead of using my extra money to take a trip to do some more investigation of a lost case, I rather spend my hard-earned money on my love by making her my wife." That warmed my heart. No one had ever put me first. That is how I could tolerate the long work hours that he was doing because I felt like his work came first. "Don't get me wrong. I like Niya but it seems like she is using you for her own personal use to help her when she gets into shit. When she was living good, she didn't call you or visit or even ask you to visit. You have been running her companies and yes, pays you well but shit you need to live your own life. I am with you because I feel like you are a beautiful person, but you are a pushover and I am tired of it. I want us to start our own life are you ready for that?" I stood there confused I did not know that Tre had been thinking that. I did not know he was thinking these things. I did like working for Aniya, but he was right as far as me worrying about her whereabouts that was not my concern, she was a grown woman. Tre was right when she was up and doing good, she did not try to contact me but now that she was in trouble, she called me. So, it made me think maybe she was good and plus I was tired of being worried about her.

"You right but I do still want to run the companies I like being a businesswoman or close to it. But you are right when do you want to leave for Vegas?" I asked and his eyes lit up. "Tonight." We packed and were on our way to Vegas. Ince we made it the next day we got married. I was ecstatic because he was the most caring, loving man in the world. No man had ever treated me like Tre had treated me. He treated me like a queen, and I was so happy to have him. Aniya was out living her life not worried about me, so I was going to do the same. I had not time for her part time friendship anymore. At first, we clicked but once we got older, she distanced herself. I understood that she was going through things and that she had problems, but she still could have been a better friend than what she was. I would never do anything to betray her and I was still going to operate her companies that I was in charge of now. All I could do was pray that her and the kids were safe because this time I could do nothing to help her I had to live my own life.

Chapter Fifteen
ANIYA

⟶ ◦ ≫ ⊹ ⊛ ⊹ ≪ ◦ ⟵

I watched my children sleep and I loved the way that their bodies moved up and down. That meant life. I kept wondering what had happened to Rashad's body? I wanted out of this damn apartment and Al Richards was taking too long getting me out of here. I walked back into my room where there was just a bed and television. I decided to write Mya I had not contacted her in a while. Dear Mya, I know you have been killing yourself worrying about the kids and I but we are okay honey. I hope that you and Tre are not trying to figure my situation out because I have things under control. Thank you for being a great friend and assistant. I feel as if I have burdened you guys as much as it is. I love the way that you care about me and I care about you to my friend but it's like I have my own life and I want you to live yours. I know that if something was to happen that you would take care of my kids and that you would make sure they were alright. I keep saying that because I really want you to know that I trust you and even if you hate me or mad at me that you are important to me and to please get my kids from wherever they are. I had tears falling from my eyes by this time, but I just wanted her to know that I trusted her. And in any event that I do not make it out of this situation then I want you to take over all of my companies they are all yours. Show Susan this letter to let her know if anything happens to me. I am leaving everything to you so that you would have all the means to take care of my kids. She knows that all my accounts should be handed to my children once they reach the age of twenty-five and it should be split amongst the both of them. I don't know why my friend, but I feel as if I am living in my last days. Love you always Aniya I started crying so hard I really did feel like things were not going good for me. I don't know I just had a feeling in the pit of my stomach that something was going to go wrong. After I wrapped up the letter I got on my knees and said a prayer. "Dear Father God please protect my children against whatever evil is going to get me. Forgive me for my sins and please open your heart to me. I love you Father God and I accept you as my savior." Before I could finish my prayer, I heard a knock at the door. It scared me something horrible. As I walked to the door, I was a nervous wreck I did not know who it could have been. I looked out the peephole to find Dale standing at the door. I opened the door and he looked shaken up. "I have to get you guys out of here" he said as he hurriedly walked in. My heart started pumping fast and I moved faster. "Word is that someone knows this location and is coming to get you, so we have to move fast." I ran back to the room and woke my kids up out of their sleep. I felt bad as they whined, and Deena did not want to get up. We had kept our clothes in suitcases. I tried to grab the suitcases, but Dale screamed at me. "We have no time for that let's go now!" Deena had started crying and I really did not have time for the dramatics. Malcolm was ready for whatever. He held his sister's hand tight. We started walking out of the house. I walked next to him and put the letter in his hand and whispered. "If anything happens to me you give this to the police so that you can go with Mya. No matter what you do not let your sister hand go okay." I said as I braced myself for the worst. He nodded his head and I saw the tears in the corner of his eyes. I know he wanted to cry but he was holding it in to not disappoint me. He wanted to cry but he wanted to be a strong man. This shit had really taken over my world. This time I really should have just walked away. I was too busy killing people without any remorse. I did not know what was going to happen but when I saw the black van pull up in front of us as we made our way to the curb I almost pissed in my pants. When the front door of the van flew open and I saw that it was Crenshaw I was shocked but relieved. Finally, Mr. Richards had sent reinforcement. I really did like Dale, but he was in the way. I hadn't thought out my plan with my children being with me but as soon as the other guy let off the round and shot Dale in his head and we watched as his brains flew out the back of his head I regretted it. Deena instantly started screaming. I grabbed her and picked her up and grabbed Malcolm hand. We ran to the van and got in. Crenshaw and the other guy sped off. I was trying my hardest to comfort Deena in the back of the van and ensure her that everything was going to be okay. Malcolm had not said anything, and I kept shaking him to make sure he was alright. It was just too much for a twelve and ten-year old to witness. At that moment I was ashamed of myself as a mother. I should have just worked with the cops and none of this would have happened. I had introduced my children to death, and I did not know how they would take it. We had been driving for hours and I did not know where they were taking us. The back of the van had no windows and to be honest I was a bit afraid. I did not know if Crenshaw was on my side or if he was going to turn on me. Hell, I did not even know if Mr. Richards was on my side but I would soon find out. The kids and I had fallen asleep and we were awaken, by someone shaking me awake. It was the other guy who was with Crenshaw. He was a Mexican with dark eyes. He told me to stand up and he did not have an accent. I stood and he walked us to this building that looked like a warehouse. As we walked through the dark building I wondered where Crenshaw was. He led us into this room where Mr. Richards was seated. The Mexican man grabbed me by the back of my hair so that I could not move my head. "What the fuck are you doing?" I questioned. I knew what was going but I did not want to admit it to myself. "Shut up bitch" the Mexican guy spat. I wanted to shoot him in his fucking face and to top it off he was musty as hell. Ugh he disgusted me. Mr. Richards stood and walked towards me. I wanted to see what my kids were doing but I could not turn my head. "Bitch you try to snitch on me then tell me that you will not do it if I pay you." He slapped me hard across my face. Malcolm screamed for me and I heard Deena start crying. "Don't worry baby I am okay." I said to comfort them. "Close your eyes" That slap wasn't shit Hakeem hit me harder than he had. I just looked at him with pure fucking hate. I knew that he had turned on me and it was all my fault I should have never called him, but my stupid ass thought that I was doing something. I wasn't doing shit but risking my kid's life. He slapped me again and I could hear my kids still crying. "Please don't hurt my kids that is all I ask of you." Mr. Richards and the Mexican guy started laughing. I did not think shit was funny so I did not see the humor in asking for my kids to be let go. "You can't ask me shit bitch! You try to snitch on me!" And he slapped me again. I was tired of his ass hitting me and if it wasn't for my kids, I would have kicked him right in his face. It was nothing to me to get out of this predicament, but I was not sure where I was at. Not only did I not know where I was, but I didn't have a gun neither. I was assed, out and I had two small people who lives where in my hands, so I had to play it smart. "Crenshaw" Mr. Richards spoke into a walkie talkie "come get these dirty ass kids." The nerve of him to call my kids dirty oooh if I ever got out of this, I was going to bring hell to Mr. Richards. The nerve of this old ass bastard to disrespect my kids. He wanted to get under my skin, but I was not going to let him. Crenshaw walked in and grabbed my kids. For some reason when he did, I felt a sense of relief. He did not look at me or anything he just grabbed them and kept walking. "Now that we got those brats out the way time to have fun." Mr. Richards said with the most sinister smile I had ever seen.

Broken 3

Chapter Sixteen
ANIYA

"I love you Niya," Hakeem said to me and it took me by surprise. I looked up at him and his pretty brown eyes were so beautiful, so inviting, so loving. "I love you too baby." I puckered my lips and closed my eyes. I felt his soft lips on mine. When I opened my eyes he was gone and I was still in a fucked up situation. I loved Hakeem so much yet hated him for what he put me through. I didn't know why I kept dreaming of him. Mr. Richards had done a number on me and I was tired. My back was hurting because he had been beating me ever since he had taken my kids away. I woke up and could barely move. He still had me in the warehouse, and I was in a big empty space with a dirty mattress on the floor. I was laying on the mattress trying to give my back some relief. After Crenshaw had come to get my kids it was on from there. Mr. Richards punched me dead in my face. I had not felt a blow like that since Hakeem. I was not accustomed to the beatings anymore. I let out a loud scream and he jumped back on me with another punch. "You shut the fuck up you nasty bitch!" I was down on the ground now and I could barely move ugh I hated myself for this shit. I jumped up though because I thought that if I could at least fight back I could get my kids. Only thing about fighting is you have to have the energy. I threw a back kick to the Mexican man he grabbed my foot in mid-air. He held on to it and the look of shock came over his face. "Oh, this bitch is trying to fight back" he then laughed. He pushed me down and they both started to kick me all over my body. I was screaming out in pain and I just wanted someone to save me. I thought that maybe Crenshaw would walk in and help but he never did. I was crying and my body was hurting badly. After what seemed like decades, they stopped the assault. I was on the floor crying my eyes out. "Shut the fuck up!" Mr. Richards screamed. He scared me so bad that I knew to shut up. I thought that they were going to get back to beating me but instead the Mexican guy grabbed both my arms and dragged me through the warehouse. I was not saying anything, but I was kicking my feet. I did not have on any shoes anymore and the ground was cold. He stopped at the big room and he threw me on the bed. I knew what was next I was not new to this. Instant flashbacks of James invaded my mind as tears poured out my eyes. He climbed on top of me and kissed my neck. "You so fucking fine" he said kissing me. He was sick this muthafucka had kidnapped me and had the nerve to think that I was cute. He was insane. "If I am so fine then why are you beating me?" I asked as tears ran down my face. "It's just business baby." He replied. He pulled down my pants as he pinned my body down with his body. I was squirming and trying to get away. I could not endure this! I could not get raped! My mind was in panic and I screamed the only thing that I could think of. "I have herpes!" I lied. He jumped up off me. "You a nasty bitch!" He yelled and kicked me in my pussy. The impact of the kick hurt, but it was nothing compared to the hurt of rape. I hurriedly pulled up my pants. He left and after a while I drifted off to sleep and now here I was in a dark, dreary room wondering what I was going to do. I did not know where I was, I had no phone, and no one knew where I was. I was trying my hardest to believe that everything would work out fine. I was in a bad situation and I did not know what was going to be my next move.

Chapter Seventeen
CRENSHAW

⚬·❯❯❯⟨⊙⟩❮❮❮·⚬

I knew what my Uncle had planned for Aniya and her kids and I was trying my hardest to get her out of the situation. My Uncle had been under investigation for years and when he found out who was testifying it was over for their life. I had been murdering for him for years. I had been an Assassin before for the nigga Montre, but it was not what I wanted to do. I got in the drug game and did murders on the side for my Uncle. I had no idea that Aniya was going to testify though. When she called him and told him he gave me the order whenever we found out where she was then we would get her, kill her son, and sell her and her daughter to the sex trade. I did not know where her husband was. I had gone to their house to see if

I could talk to him. I wanted him to help his wife out of this situation plus that is who my uncle wanted anyways. That nigga Rashad had gone missing without a trace. I decided to call him because no one had seen him. "Hello." "Aye this Rashad?" I asked. There was a pause "why? Who the fuck is this?" "This Crenshaw Al's nephew you know your wife is in witness protection and plan on testifying against my Uncle." He started laughing "for real how you know?" "She called. But ay man my uncle is going to kill her and her kids. Once she sends her location that is his plan." I let him know what was going on this was not a joke. "What?" He asked. "Look she cool. I don't want to kill her." I told him the truth. There was a long pause and I thought for a minute he hung up, "hello." "Yeeeahh!" He sighed. "Don't kill her then I don't know what the fuck to tell you." I looked down at the phone. This nigga really did not give a fuck about her. "I'm not. I need somewhere to take her." That was halfway the truth I also wanted his location so that I could kill him. "Okay look just hit me up when you get her." That's what the nigga said but when I called him to let him know that I had them he didn't answer. I looked at the children's faces. I couldn't let this happen to them. I called my sister Lucinda she would hold them until I got to Aniya then I would figure things out from there. That is where I went when my uncle told me to take them. He thought they were being killed and exchanged for money. I had other plans. I had dropped the kids off to my sister right away and made my way back to the warehouse where my uncle was keeping Aniya. Before I made it back to the warehouse my sister called me and told me that Aniya's son had a note from his mother saying that her friend Mya would take care of the kids. I told my sister to get ghost and take them wherever they had to go. When I got back to the warehouse Uncle Al called me in his office. "Nephew where is the little girl?" He had a grimace look on his face. I looked at him confused "what little girl?" "The bitch! Her daughter! Where is she?" He asked pointing to the door. He was sitting in the office of the warehouse where we had taken Aniya. I wanted to check on her, but my cousin Jeff was lurking outside her door. I had heard him saying how fine Aniya was and I was hoping that he didn't do anything to her. "Oh, I killed her," I thought quickly. He jumped up "you killed her no! No!" He screamed. I played dumb, "what's up unc?" "I told you don't kill the girl! She was going to get sold to the highest bidder!" His voice was loud, and I could tell he was angry. "Oh, shit well I didn't hear that part." I lied I know he wanted me to keep the little girl alive. I did but he would never know. I did not like that fact that he wanted to sell that little girl to be a whore. "Fuck!" He cursed loudly. That was my cue to get out of there. I wanted to go see Aniya, but I would have to wait for the right time. I went home and waited for my sister to give me a call back. She let me know that she had made that move to drop the kids off. I thanked her and tried to call Rashad again. This time it went directly to the voicemail. I shook my head, I had to get Aniya out of this shit. It was crazy that I was feeling this way, but I was willing to risk it all. I knew she was good person and the vibe that we had was indescribable. A couple of days later Uncle Al called and told me that him and Jeff were going to be gone and that I needed to keep an eye on Aniya. I jumped up and grabbed some food for her. I needed to see her. The plans had changed. Instead of killing her Uncle Al wanted her to suffer. He had told me that she would be sold any day now. I had to devise a plan to get her out of there. Right now I just needed to feed her and know that she was okay.

Chapter Eighteen
ANIYA

—————⊙◦≫≫⊛⊛⊗⊛⊗≪≪◦⊙—————

I thought that the Mexican man or Mr. Richards were going to come and do something to me, but they didn't. I was hungry and thirsty and to be honest I wanted to see them so that they could feed me at least. The room that I was in was stinking so bad from my bad odor. I knew that the day was ending, and I was tired I lay back on the bed and drifted off to sleep. As I walked into the dimly lit room there was candles everywhere. I smiled as Trey Songz blared through the speakers. The round table was set up for two. I sat down at the table and smelled the twelve dozen red roses. They were beautiful. The plate before me had a silver cover and I could not wait to see what meal was prepared inside. I heard footsteps approaching and I knew that I was not alone. The tan white hands that took a hold of my shoulders felt familiar. Lips kissed the back of my neck and I could smell his cologne. I closed my eyes as I allowed Bruce to plant warm kisses on the nape of my neck. I needed to tell him I was sorry for what had happened. I jumped out of the seat and quickly turned around. "Look Bruce…" I began but I quickly jumped back when I saw the terror before me. I stumbled over the chair. It was Bruce with his beautiful blue eyes staring back at me. In the middle of his head was a big hole that I could see through. I was frozen in fear. He reached out and tried to touch me. I jumped and it was back to reality. When I looked up it was Crenshaw smiling at me with those beautiful brown eyes. I did not know what was going on, but I was hoping like hell he was not going to kill me.

Chapter Nineteen
ANIYA

He looked at me with those beautiful eyes. Damn he looked like Hakeem. I looked at him and turned my head I had nothing to say. Those same innocent eyes that I had stared into for five years had beat me. Those eyes that danced over me with love had also bore down on me with hatred. Crenshaw wasn't Hakeem and I needed answers. I had questions and Crenshaw was going to give me some answers. I hadn't talked in days. "Where the fuck is my kids?" I tried to scream but I could barely speak. He just looked at me and he could tell I was in pain he handed me the glass of water. I drank it in a hurry. As soon as the ice cold, water hit my belly it brought sharp piercing pains through my stomach.

I screamed out and doubled over in pain. "Arrggh! Did you put something in this?" I asked through clenched teeth it was like a thousand razors had hit my insides. "No" he said whispering "you haven't drunk anything in a while, so it hurts. Drink some more." Once he thought I had enough he gave me a sandwich and a bag of chips. "Here eat this" he said. I looked up at him and ate the food. He did not say anything as he watched me eat that food. I had stuffed my face I was so hungry. I had never been starved or went without food, so this was a hard thing for me to do. As I ate, I felt the tears of shame fall from my eyes. I had never gone through anything like this before. Although Hakeem would beat me, he would never deprive me of food or something to drink. After I finished, he started talking. "Look baby girl your kids are okay. Your son gave me that letter and I had them taken to your friend's house in Wisconsin." He said looking sincere. I did not know what to say because I was not expecting him to say that. Inside I was happy as hell and I wanted to jump for joy. My babies were safe. I knew one thing for sure was that Mya would take care of my babies her and Tre. They would raise them right and they would be alright. If I wasn't in a fucked up, predicament right now then I would have the biggest smile on my face. "Look I never wanted to leave but I had to get your kids away first. I like you Niya you are a real sweet lady. I knew my uncle was going to beat and torture you. He asked me to come and get you with the help of my cousin Jeff. I said yes because I wanted to help you. I don't have a plan, but I am working on one to get you out of this situation. Do you know where your husband is?" I shook my head no. He looked at me with sympathy. "I am going to try to get you out here" he said and left. I didn't know what to believe when it came to Crenshaw. That dream that I had about Bruce, it made me feel guilty. Maybe this was my payback for all the bad things that I had done. All I could do was be grateful that he had given me food and water. It had been three days and I had not had anything to drink or eat. I did not know if they had forgotten about me or what, but I was near death. I was blanking in and out of consciousness I was so weak. My stomach felt like it no longer existed. My head hurt so bad and when I opened my mouth the saliva had dried up to the point my throat hurt. I just prayed that this would be over soon. I had given up I was not longer in a fighting mood. All I wanted to do was die. I fell asleep in hopes that I would not wake up. I walked down a long, dark hall I heard footsteps. I thought they were mine but when I stopped, I could still hear them. "Aniya," the voice spoke. I turned around and my heart skipped a beat it was Hakeem. "Hakeem why did you leave me?" He looked at me and the smile turned into a frown. He was hurting, I was hurting. It was all his fault! If he had been the man that he was supposed to be then I would not be going through this. Our children would not be going through this. I ran to him and started hitting him. I slapped his face and he did nothing. I beat his chest and after a minute I just collapsed in his arms and cried. He held me, he held me like he loved me, he held me like he cared, he held me like he missed me, he held me and for a minute I could picture him here with me and just like that he was gone. I opened my eyes and I was crying. I didn't even know that I could still produce tears. I heard someone in the room, and I hoped that it was not Mr. Richards nor the Mexican man to beat on me. They had not messed with me since that first day and I was happy about that. To my surprise it was Crenshaw I had not seen him since the day he fed me and gave me something to drink. He walked over to me. He looked at me with sadness in his eyes. It hurt him to see me hurting I knew it. "Come on shawty I am about to get you out of here." He said and he picked me up. I had lost some weight, but I knew that the dead weight of my body was hard to pick up. He struggled with me at first. I don't know if it was my weight or the stink that was coming from my body but he kept right on moving. Where they had me it was a long walk to the outside. After we made it to the outdoors the breath of fresh air was heavenly, and I breathed deep. To my surprise the sun was shining bright and the sky was blue. I guess being with no sunlight I imagined the outside would look as dark as I felt. I knew that without Crenshaw I would have died because there was no way in hell that I could have gotten out of there by myself. I did not have the strength to do it. The walk that we took to get out of the building was long and I was weak from being starved. He threw me in his car, and we drove away. I knew it was his car because I had been in it enough times. He had a silver 2015 Infiniti Q70 and it drove like a dream. Crenshaw didn't say anything as we drove away from that warehouse. I was too weak to talk, I closed my eyes and drifted off to sleep. "Crenshaw where are you taking me?" I laughed. I had gotten tired of sitting in the house waiting for Rashad all night. I was not about to sit up at the club neither because I was feeling uncomfortable. It was like he did not want me there because he wanted to do his dirt. Rashad would constantly ask me don't you want to go lay down or don't you want to spend time with the kids. Hell, no I didn't they were sleep and anytime I needed a babysitter Mrs. Thompson would make sure to come and watch them. She should I was paying their mortgage and had gotten them out of debt. Rashad knew he wanted to be a hoe and he did not want me to see it. I would usually sit and sip on my Hennessy but tonight I did not feel like entertaining the muthafucka. Plus, Crenshaw had texted me and let me know that he was in town. I was excited but I was not going to let him know. "Come on you know that I am a good guy so let's just have fun together stop worrying and get in the car." I had told him to come get me that night. When he came, I was so damn scared that I tried to back out. He was looking too good to me. He had on a black Polo shirt and I could smell his Usher cologne as soon as he stepped outside the car. You know how that is when a man smells good the panties come off and right now my Victoria's Secret panties were dripping just from the sight of him. Although I was mad at Rashad, I would never cheat on him I loved the man too much. I got in the car reluctantly and sat in the passenger's side. I had on a dress that was rose red and it had no sleeves. The dress fell right above my knees. I had decided to wear my rose red sling backs to match and I had my little matching handbag. I had two Goddess braids in my hair, and I knew that I was looking good because my makeup was flawless. My body was smelling good because I had on some of Beyonce's Heat on and the heat was turned up. Crenshaw was staring at me smiling I knew he wanted me. From having so many conversations with Crenshaw I had learned a lot about him. He was a sweet guy although he did run dope for his uncle. He had hopes and dreams. He wanted to own his own barbershop. He was helping his sister with her kids because their father had gotten killed. It was just him and her and he loved his sister dearly. To my surprise Crenshaw was playing some blues Johnnie Taylor "my last two dollars" and I burst out laughing. What did this young boy know about the blues? "What's so funny?" He asked. I had to catch my breath before I answered him. His eyebrows were not frowned up and he looked so good and so young. "Really Crenshaw my last two dollars what do you know about that?" He pulled off, "I know a lot about that. I keep telling you there is more to me than this gangsta demeanor that you see little lady. I just wish you wasn't married because for real I would make you my lady." I just sat there in silence. Crenshaw and I had been texting back and forth. This was the first time we hung out. I didn't tell him about my marital problems because as far as I was concerned, I didn't have any marital issues. I had never caught Rashad with any one all I had was accusations and suspicions. And to assume I did not because you know what they say when you assume you make an ass out of you. I would throw shit out there to let him know that I was watching. Whenever I felt like he was doing something I would speak on it and he would make that problem disappear. I knew Rashad loved me and I knew that he wanted to keep our family together. He loved my kids. He took them out more than I did. He bought them clothes and whatever they needed. He was their father and I loved how he came in and took over when he didn't have too. That was something many men did not do. They could care less that a woman had kids they would dog her, and her kids and Rashad did not do that. We parked in an empty lot. There were lights from the streetlamps, but it still was creepy. I looked over at Crenshaw as he turned off the car. I was ready to punch his ass if he was on some creepy shit. I should have brought my gun. "Niya I don't know what it is about you but when I saw you on the plane that day. I just couldn't get you out of my head. I saw you with Bruce and I was going to take you from him, but I got sidetracked with personal things in my life. So, when I saw you again,

I knew I had to get in your good graces. I know you married but I knew that if you were happy you wouldn't be here with me." He paused for a moment and looked away and I swore I could see a tear about to drop from his eyes. This man was smitten over me that was great, but I still wasn't falling for his shit. I had fell too many times and I did not like where I always ended. "I just want to give you a chance to know me. The real me. Crenshaw Lamont Richards can you do that for me?" I shook my head yes. I was damn near in tears, but I held them in. He turned the music on Trey Songz "Already Taken" song came on. He started singing and he had a beautiful voice. Who would have known this thug had the voice of an angel I swayed to the music and grabbed his hand. We got out the car and we danced to the sweet sound of his voice. That night I had fell in love with Crenshaw and I did not even realize it. The next day I was singing the song to Rashad. It was partly because I was thinking of Crenshaw and it was also because that is what he needed to tell those bitches. He was sitting in the living room watching television and I sat down and started singing Every night up in the club getting money with the thugs thought I never fall in love And there was you Rashad didn't even flinch he just looked at me and said, "damn baby I love when you sing to me." He was such an asshole. He knew what I was trying to say, and he knew damn well I couldn't sing. That was Crenshaw's and I first date, but it wasn't our last. We never had sex he was a gentlemen just like now.

Chapter Twenty
CRENSHAW

S hawty and I had history so maybe that was one reason why I felt the need to rescue her. Or maybe it was because she was beautiful. Or maybe it was because I was getting soft whatever it was it just felt right. I watched as Aniya slept as I drove to our destination. She was beautiful although she smelled awful. I loved the way her big lips looked puckered out as she slept. When I first saw Aniya I peeped her and thought she was good looking. I kept seeing her but that day at the Lennox Mall it just felt right and comfortable. I initially didn't want to take it there with her but every time I saw her, she looked so unhappy. That smile on her face didn't mean shit to me her eyes looked unhappy. That is why that day in the Mall I made sure to make her smile, make her laugh. I didn't know that I would think about that smile and that cute laugh every day until then. At night I would think about the way that she would laugh and burp at the same time. She was beautiful yet tainted. I knew she was tainted it was just something about the way she looked. I never knew what she had been through but from one killer to another I knew that Aniya had killed. I don't know why I had never noticed it before, but I saw it when Jeff killed that cop Dale. She didn't even flinch. Most people would have been scared shitless. She picked her daughter up and grabbed her son and kept on moving. She was a woman who had experienced death before. I got a call it was from Uncle Al, but I didn't answer I just looked down at the phone. I know why he was calling. I grabbed the phone and just decided to shut it off. I didn't know how I was going to explain or even if I needed to explain but I wasn't ready to do neither. Her husband had changed his phone number, so I had to make other plans. The plan was to take Aniya and her kids to her husband, but he changed his number. Once I found out that the kids had a place to go it was just Aniya. I knew she didn't want to face it, but she had to play dead or something until the cops found my Uncle and could hold a case against him. This was a must because he was going to sell her or kill her. I had to come up with a lie to where I was because Uncle Al had told me to go to the house to watch Aniya while they went and handled some business. He was going to want an explanation on where she went. I did not know what I was going to say right now so I ignored his calls. I know that it is fucked up how I am betraying my Uncle, but he is heartless and don't give a fuck about no one. Yes, he had come to get me out of the predicament that I was in. That does not change all the dirty shit I have witnessed him do. It was something about Aniya that just made me want to save her. She would call me, and I could hear the tears in her voice, but she always played it off. I would ask her if something was wrong and she would deny it. Those dates and the times we spent together were the happiest times I had with a woman. After getting played by my ex Talia and E I didn't care too much for women. My ex Talia had lied to me. The entire time she was pregnant she had me thinking that I was the Father. The day that the boy was born I told her I wanted to name the boy after me. I had been to the ultrasounds, doctor visits, held her hand while she pushed and cut the umbilical cord. So, when the lady came in to do the name and the social security card I let the woman know I wanted the baby to be named after me. "Ma'am I would like for my son to be a junior." I told the woman. She was a pretty white woman with short blond hair. She smiled at me I was a proud father and as soon as he got a name, I was going to get it tatted on my chest. "Wait Crenshaw we shouldn't do that." Talia said she was still sore from giving birth. "What you mean we shouldn't do that?" We had not discussed names every time I brought it up Talia would change the subject. I thought that she just didn't want to discuss it at that time. It was time now the baby was born. "I will leave you two to talk. Just give me a call when you have decided." She left the paperwork on the bed as she left out. I turned to Talia and she had tears sliding down her face. I knew it right then and there that the baby wasn't mine "he ain't mine, is he?" I asked. "I don't know" she said through tears. I knew the shit was too good to be true. I got up and she screamed my name "Crenshaw wait!" I kept walking I was not in the mood she had lied to me for nine months. As I left, I saw the doctors wheeling my little man back to the room. He had gone to go get circumcised I wanted to go to the little guy and kiss him, but it was too much. Tears rolled down my face as I left the hospital my hopes of becoming a father was over. Two months later we had the paternity test done. I did not know who the other guy was, but it must have been his baby because he sure in the hell wasn't mine. I was heartbroken. I had been told when I was younger that I couldn't have kids. When I found out that Talia was pregnant I felt that miracles did happen, I was wrong.

Chapter Twenty-One
ANIYA

The car came to a stop and I jumped out of my sleep. I had slept the entire ride and I did not know where we were, but I felt safe with Crenshaw. It was a hotel and apparently Crenshaw already had the room. As we got into the elevator he was looking around and I was looking forward. I hated we had to get on the elevator because my body odor was unbearable. Crenshaw had kept the windows rolled down I know he smelled me. "Run you some bath water." He said as soon as we got in the room. I would have taken offense had I not smelled like the zoo. His hazel brown eyes sparkled, and he smelled so good. I didn't say anything I just turned and walked to the bathroom hell I was tired of smelling myself. The bathtub was already clean, but I cleaned it again and ran me some hot water. I was so thankful that Mexican man did not rape me. I was glad that I had thought of something because I do not think that my mental state could take anymore abuse. I looked down at my panties and they were pink. I was on to be on my period that was fucked up. I stripped out of my clothes that I was in. They were sticky and dirty, and the odor was treacherous. I was ashamed to be in Crenshaw's presence because he smelled so good. I know under the circumstances my mind should have been on something else, but I couldn't help but feel dirty and ugly. My hair was a mess. I was musty the smell from my vagina was going to take hours to wash away and on top of that I was coming down on my period. This was not a good look on me. My breath stunk the smell that came out of my lips when I opened my mouth was nasty. While I was held captive, I would piss in a cup in the corner and I even shitted in the corner of that room. I was ashamed of myself. I hadn't had any food or drink, so the bathroom breaks were not frequent. I lay my head back in the tub and watched as the clear water turned gray. I shook my head I was that damn dirty. I stepped out the tub and let the water out. I washed the tub out again and ran some more water. It was better I relaxed in the hot tub and closed my eyes I wonder what my kids had been doing. I missed they ass like crazy and I was angry that I had let this shit happen. I heard a knock on the bathroom door, and I jumped out of my sleep. Damn I kept dozing off. "Come in," I said. I knew it could only be Crenshaw. I did not care about him seeing me naked hell he had smelled my bad body odor so what could he say about my body. He came in and looked at me. You could tell he liked what he saw he licked his lips and smiled. This man looked too much like Hakeem that was the same thing that Hakeem would do. He would walk in while I was in the tub and lick his lips and smile with that same smile. "I got you some clothes. Some panties and bras and stuff so you can be comfortable I got you some hygiene stuff to because you were funky." He joked. I instantly started crying. "I was just kidding Niya don't cry." He kneeled down next to me. He smelled so good and looked so good I wanted to kiss him, but I had not brushed my teeth. I started laughing at the thought. He looked at me like I had lost my mind. For someone who had just gone through so much bullshit I think that he understood because he started laughing too. "Did you get me some pads?" "No why would I get those?" He got up from his knees and was placing the things in the bathroom. "Well I am on my period so could you go get some pads for me please?" He looked at me crazy. Then he thought about it and headed out the door. I dried myself off and put on the Jergens lotion he had bought. I put on the underwear and put folded up some tissue in them. This would have to do until he came back. As I grabbed the bra, I was surprised that he got my bra size correct 34 C. I put on the gray jogging pants he bought with the t shirt. They were too big but comfortable. I brushed my teeth about three times and used the mouth wash. I combed through my hair it was still short, but it looked crazy. It had grown back in the places that were supposed to be tapered. I grabbed the jam that Crenshaw bought and slicked my hair down. I was finally decent I thought to myself. I can't look too fly after I just went through all that bullshit. I went out and saw that he had bought some food. It was some Zaxby. I loved Zaxby I did not know if the food was for me or him, but I fucked them wings and chicken tenders up. It was hard to eat at first but once that good food touched the bottom of my stomach it felt so good that my hunger pain came back. I had been so hungry that my body had stopped thinking about food. I fell asleep right after. That chicken really hit the spot. When Crenshaw came back, he woke me up. I was tired and weak. "Here go your pads woman" he threw the bag at me. I went to the bathroom and put the pad on I was happy that the flow was not heavy. I walked back into the room and Crenshaw was looking at the Zaxby's bag. He looked at me. "Niya was you that hungry that you had to eat my food too? You knew that one of them was mine." "I am sorry, but I was hungry." I put my head down in shame. To my surprise he started laughing. "You wasn't that damn hungry." He was smiling and that made me smile. "Damn I guess I will order me some room service don't make no damn sense." He ordered him some room service and I did too I was still hungry. It was going to be a minute before they came, so he got in the shower. I did not know what was going to happen because we had not really talked about anything. I was too busy sleeping to even focus on the task at hand but now that I had got my rest I was focused and ready for what was next. The room service came quicker than I thought, and I grabbed the food. I made sure to wait for Crenshaw. He exited the bathroom ten minutes later and looked at the table. "When did they come bring this food?" He asked as he started throwing on his clothes and grabbing shit. He was making me scared so I started putting on my shoes. He wasn't about to leave me I was going where he was going. "About ten minutes ago," I said doing what he was doing. "Damn we got about twenty minutes. Get the shit out the bathroom and let's go," he headed out the door. I was scared I did not know what was going on. All we did was get room service. I knew that he might be hungry, so I grabbed the plate too. I threw my hygiene stuff in the bag that it came in and ran out the door. Crenshaw was already at the running car waiting outside of it. He was looking around. I hopped in the car and he did the same and sped off. "Damn I am sorry I should have told you not to answer the door, but I did not think they would bring the food that fast." He hit the steering wheel "Damn!" I did not know what was going on, but I was scared. I started crying. "Don't cry Niya and thanks for grabbing the food for me." He smiled that smile. It made me stop crying. I fed him his burger while he drove. I felt bad for eating his food and then I was the reason we had to leave the hotel. We were on the road for about an hour or so when we reached another hotel. We got out he checked us in. We went to the room. He sat me down and explained everything it was worse than I had that. "My uncle Mr. Richards he was going to sell you to the sex trade. He was going to kill your son and sell your daughter. I dropped them off at my sister's house and she said that your son gave her a note and they are now safe with your friend in Wisconsin. I need for you to call your friend and tell her that your kid's names need to be changed asap. If my uncle finds out that I did not kill them then he will find them and do what he set out to do. I know I scared you back there, but I think that I was being followed. I think that my uncle is skeptical, and he thinks that I took you. I did not tell them I took you they think that I am out looking for you. Look Niya I care about and I do not want to hurt you." I jumped up and hugged him. If they found out that Crenshaw was against them then they would try to kill him too. I kissed him and it felt so good. I put my tongue in his mouth and found his tongue. He pulled me off him. I felt rejected. "Calm down lady. Look we are safe now we are out of Georgia we are in Oxford, Alabama and they will not be looking for us here. I do not know for sure if they saw you back at that hotel, but they knew I was staying in that room. I am going to stay here with you tonight. Tomorrow I have to head back to Georgia to make it look good. After that we will leave and go far away." "What about my kids?" I asked crying. "You have to wait for all of that Niya. Right now, where they are is the safest place. I don't know where your husband is, but he made himself ghost. They looking for him too and I know that they haven't found him yet." I choked at the mention of Rashad I was going through so much I had forgotten the awful deed I had done. That night I lay in bed and cried. I had killed Rashad. Shit if I had not then he still would have been somewhere dead. We should have never fucked with Mr. Richards. I knew I was wrong. It was like I had made all the wrong choices and now it was coming back to me. I had lost my children I knew that Mya would take good care of them, but it still hurt that I would not be in their lives.

Chapter Twenty-Two
CRENSHAW

I was on the road again. While Aniya got in the shower, I went back to meet my Uncle. It was an hour drive back. I met him at the warehouse. I had not answered my phone yet, but I knew where he would be and how long he would wait. He looked up at me, him, and my cousin Jeff. They were sitting in the office once again. As soon as I walked in the door Jeff punched me in the stomach. I doubled over in pain. As I grabbed my stomach, I also grabbed my Glock. I rose up with my pistol pointed. "What the fuck is going on?" I yelled. "You tell me! The girl is gone under your watch!" Uncle Al yelled. "You not answering your phone! Where have you been?" "What the fuck you mean?" I ran to the room where they had Aniya.

I busted through the door. "What the fuck!" I yelled I had to play it off. I ran back to the office. "Where the bitch at?" I still had my gun drawn. "You tell me! I told you to watch her!" He yelled. "You didn't get my text? I texted and told you to have Jeff look after her." I lied. "I was taking care of some business." "I didn't get a text I told you not to be texting me you know I don't know how to work that phone." I put my gun down. "Unc you gotta get technology savvy. Damn man so y'all left her here by herself? So y'all left before y'all saw me pull up? That was y'all fuck up." I let them know. Jeff shook his head like he didn't believe me. I knew I had Uncle Al though because this was not common for me to text him and he not read the message. "Fuck! You think she will go back to the police?" I asked. "I don't know." Uncle Al responded. I stood there for a second "well shit hit me up when y'all figure shit out I got money to be made." I turned to leave. "Nephew!" Uncle Al called out. "What up?" I turned around to him. "Blood is everything. You remember all I have done for you?" It was a question yet also a threat. "Of course." "Don't ever cross me." I didn't say anything as I walked to my car. I breathed in deeply once I drove away from the warehouse. I was scared that he was going to have one of his killer's shoot me in the car, but he didn't. I had suspicions that he was having people follow me, but I couldn't place them. I had decided to keep Aniya safe until Unc was behind bars or dead. I didn't know where her punk ass husband was. I was hoping that he came to me before he came to Uncle Al because that was Aniya's mistake. The day that Aniya called Unc I was visiting him in his home. He was acting as if everything was good. He was acting like nothing had changed but it had. He was being investigated again. The Feds investigation was taking long because they wanted a witness. Unc would have me kill whoever he thought had turned against him. Usually he was right and this time it happened to be Rashad. We were sitting watching the game when Unc phone rang. "Hello," he picked it up and put it on speaker. "Mr. Richards hi this is Aniya, Rashad's wife." Aniya's voice was muffled and scared. "Yes, what is it?" "The Feds have got me and the want me to testify but I am not going to do it." She got right to the point. I shook my head because that was a death sentence. "Oh, so you saying they have you right now? Where are you?" He asked getting anxious. I had turned the television on mute. I couldn't believe this girl had called the person who she was supposed to snitching out. Her husband had not told her shit about the game. If you are in witness protection, then you are not supposed to reveal your location. No matter if you think the person who you are going to testify against is for you. Once you are in custody then a muthafucka don't care you are a snitch as far as they are concerned. Unc hung up from her and looked at me "I found the rat now it is time to get rid of her." "Didn't she say she wasn't going to snitch though?" I questioned like I didn't know the game. "She had to tell them something don't be stupid Crenshaw they are keeping her for a reason." I nodded my head and went along with everything. The whole set up I was there tagging along to find out information. I was hoping that Aniya would not tell Unc her exact location. He located her in no time once he put a tracer on the phone. I didn't know how we were going to get out of this situation but from now on I was leading because Aniya did not know what she was doing.

Chapter Twenty – Three
MYA

———— ∞»❂«∞ ————

I had two surprises waiting on me when I got back. Malcolm and Deena were at the house when Tre and I arrived back from Las Vegas. Good thing we had cut our trip a bit short. I did not know how long they had been here, but I was happy to see them. Malcolm had remembered that I kept a spare key under the potted plant on my porch. I was happy that he paid attention to what I had told him. He handed me the letter that Aniya had wrote me and I went in my room. I was in tears I knew that she was dead. I started crying and Tre walked in the room. "What's the matter?" He ran to me. I handed him the letter and he shook his head. "Who gave this to you?" "Malcolm" I said through tears. He went in the room with the kids and I could hear Malcolm telling him the story about how the men had grabbed them and their Mama. He said that the one man was ordered to kill them by an old Mexican man. They thought the dude was going to kill them, but he drove them to a house with a woman. Her name was Lucinda. Lucinda was the guy who name was Crenshaw's sister. She had three kids of her own. Two boys and a girl who were about Malcolm's and Deena's age. Crenshaw was supposed to come back and drop them off somewhere. He had got held up so he told his sister to drop them off. She asked them if they had any family and Malcolm told her about me. She said that Wisconsin was a far, so she contacted her brother. He told her to make it happen and he would pay her. The next day she went to go get a rental and they hit the road. She dropped them off. They had been standing there ringing the doorbell and banging on the door. Malcolm was going to give up but then he remembered the key. He didn't want to go back because he was scared that the bad men would find them and kill them. He let himself in and went around to the front and opened the door for Deena. Once she saw that they were safely in the house she drove off. They had been here for two days before we came home. Thankfully I always kept food in the refrigerator. Tre came back into the room with me and I was crying I did not know what to do. I was a married woman now. I had to ask Tre a hard question and I just hoped that he was going to give me the response that I wanted, that I needed to hear. "So, what do you think? Do you think that we should keep them? She is my best friend, but I know that we have our lives together now." Tre grabbed my face and he wiped my tears away. "Yes, they are staying with us. I feel bad as it is. If, I, we would have just gone to Georgia like we planned and never gotten married then this would not have happened. I did want to marry you. I did think that Niya was playing around because I was not finding anything on her. Now I don't know. I know something is up and I want to get to the bottom of it." He got up and put on his pants. "I am going to the office you get them situated. It looks like they are going to be with us for now and we need to get a bigger house and things like that and them some clothes and toys. I need to find out what the fuck is going on." He threw a stack of money to me. I looked on in surprise. Tre never showed me he had this type of money. He had been working trying to get some money. He paid all the bills, so I was not expecting him to give me some money. I would not mind spending my money I had lots of money in the bank. He left out the door and I counted out the money.

He had given me four thousand dollars. I could only wonder where he had gotten this money from when we just had come from Vegas. I couldn't think about it now I had to see about Malcolm and Deena. I walked into the room and it stunk I had not noticed the odor before. I looked and they were dirty. I didn't have any clothes there for them. "If I leave you guys. Go run out and just get y'all one outfit. So that y'all could get dressed then will you guys promise me that you will not leave?" Malcolm looked at me with anger in his eyes I thought he was mad at me then they changed into hurt. "We don't have anywhere to go." I nodded my head and left. I couldn't say anything because I was close to tears and I did not want them to see me cry. I jumped in my Malibu and the tears ran down my face. These kids were without their mother and father. They had no one in the world but Tre and I. I really needed to get things straight because I was going to be the best mother to them that I could be. They did not deserve this. No child deserved to be without their parents. I quickly went to Walmart and grabbed them some things. I prayed the entire time that they would still be at my house. When I got back, I was relieved that they were still there. I gave them the clothes and underwear to put on. Deena got in the tub in the hallway and I let Malcolm come in our master bathroom. Those kids had gone through some things and they smelled like it. I was watching television waiting for them to get done. My mind was going in circles and I did not know where my thoughts began or where they ended. Tre had texted me to let me know that he had made it safely to his office. I texted him a smiley face. I was not in the mood for texting. My family did not even know that I had gotten married yet. Then I was going to have to tell them that I was taking in Niya's kids. I think they would be okay with it though because the last time I told they were here with me my parents did not say anything. I was happy that I had a good supportive family. Deena came in and I did a smell check because I wanted to make sure she was clean. I brushed her curly hair and tamed it into a ponytail. Wasn't nothing that Luster Pink Moister couldn't help. Malcolm came out of the bathroom about ten minutes later and I saw that he needed a haircut that was the first place we were going to go. We went to the barbershop first and it was a long wait. I made a mental note to never do this again this was something I would let Tre handle. I didn't have patience when I had to wait at the salon to get my hair washed and shampoo. We went and tore the mall down. I bought them so much stuff that it was a workout getting those clothes and shoes in the house. They thanked me over and over again. We had eaten while we were out, but those kids still looked hungry. I knew that Tre would be hungry and although I had not gotten any rest from my trip, I decided to cook steak, loaded potato, mixed vegetables, and some dinner rolls. I called and checked with my assistant that I had hired before I left. Janet was a white girl who was all about business. She was a red head with green eyes, and she was a bit overweight. She dressed accordingly so her size was cute on her. She was a business major and she was good at helping me run things at the companies that Niya had left me. I knew one thing I was going to keep putting her share of her money into her account. Truth was no one knew if for certain she was dead. I was hoping that she wasn't because I just could not think about my best friend being gone. I wiped the tears that were starting and made the call. Janet reassured me that everything was okay, and I told her to give me a couple of days and I would be back in the office. I had rented out a space and put my office in there. We had gotten cleaned up and was about to eat dinner when Tre walked in. I did not expect him this early. He looked beat. We ate our dinner in silence, and I told Tre to go upstairs and get some rest. He looked so tired and I knew how he felt but I could pull through because as tired as I was my mind was restless. I cleaned the kitchen and sat in the living room with Malcolm and Deena. They had been quiet since they came to me. I know they were thinking about their mother and if she was okay because those thoughts were running through my mind. I really wanted to know what my friend had been doing the past five years to be in some shit like this. I let the television watch me as I dozed off to sleep. Chapter Twenty- Four Mya It had been a month since Malcolm and Deena had come to us. They had started school and they seemed to be okay. They were like normal kids they laughed and joked and got along with other kids. If I hadn't known what they went through, then I would have never guessed they cope with things very well just like their mother. I had gotten the letter from Niya about two weeks after they came. I was so excited I tore it open I was so happy to just know that she was alive. Dear Mya, I know you are worried and right now honey I am okay. I need you to do something important for me you need to change Malcolm and Deena's name. The people know their names and Lord willing that they will not find them but changing their names would help. I love you and I love them so much I don't know when I will be able to write again but tell them I love them always. Love your best very best friend in the world, A'Niya. I cried tears that day. I told Tre about what she said in the letter and he agreed. I had to explain it to Malcolm and Deena. Malcolm understood but Deena it was hard convincing her. She wanted to know why and where was her mother? She had been holding up well but the thought of change I think scared the little girl. After about twenty minutes Malcolm was tired of it. "Look Deena shut up the whining and just go with it. I am tired of your whining it's time to grow up!" I know he did not want to be yelling at his baby sister especially saying that because she was only ten, but he got through to her. I hated having to make these kids grow up fast and think like adults, but that was the life that they had been dealt. Malcolm was overcome with joy once he knew that his mother was alive and okay. I think it gave him hope that she would come back to get them. She had come back before but this time I was not so sure but who was I to break the fella's heart. We had decided to buy a bigger house so that the kids could have their own room. Tre had closed on the house last week and he had everything packed up and boxed by the weekend. I loved the neighborhood and the schools that we lived by. I had chosen to transfer them to schools close to the house. Deena whose name now was Danity was in her last year of

Elementary school and the bus came to get her. Malcolm whose name now was Maurice was in Junior High and his school was in walking distance. I would wait for them to head off to school before I left and went to the office. I still made sure to put Niya's part of the money in her account. My sister Monica was a big help to me and when I told her about what happened to Niya she felt sad for her. My mother and father were a big help too. They were old but my father took Maurice fishing. Danity didn't like it but they said that they would find another activity for her. I had told my family that Tre and I had gotten married and that right there was another story. I mean they liked Tre, but they felt like I should have told them about the wedding. I explained to them that it was the spur of the moment and they still did not understand. I do wish that my family was there. I did not wear a wedding gown. I wore a green silk gown and Tre wore a suit. I was beautiful on my wedding day and Tre was handsome. We had some people from the hotel where we stayed come be our witness. Brenda and her boyfriend Fred were on vacation and they were from Oregon. They were a cute couple. I liked Brenda she gave me her number to keep in touch, but my life was too busy. She cried at the wedding and it made the day feel more intimate. It made me think about

Aniya's wedding and how I had cried for her happiness. When her and Rashad got married it was a little ceremony at his parent's house. They looked good together of course I was her maid of honor. Tre was Rashad's best man since his brother was in jail. Their colors were white and lavender. My lavender maid of honor dress was gorgeous but Niya's wedding dress was to die for. It fitted perfectly onto her body at the top and the bottom was a big puff. Her train was long, and Deena carried it for her. The DJ had messed up when it was time for Niya to walk out. He accidently put on "Love In this Club" by Usher. Rashad was pissed and everybody else was laughing even Niya. She was in the back cracking up. "Really this fool is fucking up." She said to me. I didn't see how she was laughing I was pissed too just like Rashad. All the man had to do was put the right song on and he couldn't do that. He finally got the right song, and everybody settled down as Case "Happily Ever After" came on. Couldn't we please be happily ever after? Couldn't we be baby Leaving you never till forever's gone. It was beautiful they said their vows. I do not remember the words that they said but I do remember the look that they gave each other. Rashad was looking into Niya's hazel brown eyes and she was looking into his gray eyes. They were lost in love. The water works started and Niya reached and grabbed my hand to comfort me. I knew she loved that man and that she would do anything for him. Rashad was a good man from what I could see. I knew that Niya deserved a good man. I did not understand what happened in those five years. There was a huge gap in between the wedding and now. My questions would be answered when the time was right.

Chapter Twenty-Five
ANIYA

I rolled off Crenshaw. We had just had sex for the third time, and I was worn out. That dick was so good. I knew he was gone have that bomb. I had finally given him the pussy since it looked like we were going to be together and that young boy had skills. The way he arched my back when he hit it from the back OOOOH! The way he ate my pussy and made my toes curl DAAAAMNNN! The way he held my waist while I rode that ten inches SHHHHIIITTT! He had saved my children and for that I put this pussy on him. I didn't even know I had those moves. My head game wasn't all that, but I know he appreciated it. I know one thing while I was sucking it, I was thinking in the back of mind damn he gone have to be gentle. He was gentle too, yet rough and he tore this kitty UP! After a while Mr. Richards had calmed down about trying to find me. Crenshaw said he think that his Uncle knew that he had me, but he was not going to tell him where we were. The FEDS had dropped the charges because they had no witnesses. They were looking for me now in connection with the killing of Dale. I don't know if they thought that I had killed him or what. I knew that they would be looking for me. The only way I knew this was because Mr. Richards had told Crenshaw. The cops had told him their witness got away and killed a FED. Little did they know they were talking to the one who had gotten him killed. We had settled in Anniston, Alabama and was renting a house from this older lady Mrs. Nixon. She was nice and we were only paying two fifty a month for the two-bedroom one story house. Although it had been a month, I missed my kids. I did not know if I would ever be able to come out of hiding. This was tearing me up and there was, times when I would just break down cry like right now. I didn't have a picture of them or anything, but their faces were embedded in my memory. "What you crying about now Amber?" It was Crenshaw. I had changed my name so that no one would know who I was. Crenshaw did not change his name because no one was looking for him. I had a 24-inch red weave in my hair with spiral curls. I never left my hair short so that no one would notice me. I had put in some green contacts to conceal my hazel brown eyes. I did what I had to do to make sure no one knew who I was. No one had mentioned Rashad's death it was like it never happened, but I know it did. Mr. Richards was back to distributing and from what Crenshaw told me Darien was back buying from him. I did not know why Darien had started back working for Mr. Richards but that was his business. Crenshaw never brought up the fact that I killed Rashad, so I guess no one knew. "I miss my kids." He came and gave me a hug. "I know you do and I told you my uncle not looking for you anymore and you can go get them." "But the FEDS are looking for me too Crenshaw." "I know and I am trying to figure out what to do about that situation too. Once I figure it out then I will tell you." I gave him a kiss a long passionate kiss. I had a strong like for Crenshaw even before this. I did not know if I loved him, but I did know that I liked him. I was still married to Rashad and I was still grieving over him. Crenshaw was a smooth guy and I liked to spend time with him. I knew that he cared about me. He was close to his uncle and I knew that betraying him hurt him deeply that is how I knew Crenshaw cared for me. He had given me a little background history on his relationship with his uncle one day when he was in town and I went to spend time with him at his hotel. He was rubbing my feet while I drank my shot of Hennessy. "My uncle been on some real fuck shit lately." I had let Crenshaw in on how his uncle was becoming sloppy and he agreed with me. Mr. Richards was the connect and he was acting like he was new to the game. Crenshaw did not appreciate that shit and neither did I. If he was sloppy that meant we were sloppy. "The nigga ain't been delivering on time. I ain't got time to be making these trips for the nigga to be having me wait last time I missed my fucking flight." I know this was not the time, but Crenshaw was turning me on with the way he was getting all rowdy. Um he was sexy I loved the way he wore those slugs in his mouth. He was so attractive, and I loved the way he was rubbing my feet. I was getting wet just with him rubbing my feet and I imagined him rubbing this pussy. He was talking business and my mind was on naughty thoughts. "Niya is you listening?" He asked. I was looking at him, but I had not heard anything. "Yeah sweetie" I said. "Your ass not listening you got your damn mind in the gutter" he laughed I did not know how he knew. "It's okay I know you want me. You can't have none of these ten inches until you divorce that pretty boy." He laughed. I knew that Crenshaw liked me. We stayed in the friend zone because I was married the man had morals. If he didn't being that I felt like Rashad was stepping out on me I would have been let Crenshaw screw me until I screamed. I know he wanted me because anytime we would be together his dick would be on hard. Every time he left, he made me wonder what female was getting what I wasn't. I wasn't complaining though because Crenshaw would get me wet and Rashad would fuck me when I got home. I would forget all about my trust issues and I would fuck him like I loved his sexy ass. I really did love Rashad he was who I was in love with. We had our issues, but I was not going to leave him. I wanted to work through our problems because I knew that if I didn't, I would regret it because Rashad was my true love. That was how I once felt but he had pushed me to the limit. The cheating was one thing that I had tried to deal with, but I couldn't. That day when I caught him fucking Trickzy I lost my mind and did the unthinkable. I wanted to take it back and if I could I would.

Chapter Twenty-Six
DARIEN

I had started back fucking with Mr. Richards because he was beneficial to what I had going on. That is the only reason I was fucking with his old ass. He was a dumb ass muthafucka if you asked me and I was ready to off his ass, but I needed to know where Aniya and her kids were. I had learned her location, but when I got to the hotel the Feds had her. I thought Mr. Richards was looking for my wife Rebecca and I. I did not know why but I sure as hell was going to find out. I had never dealt with the unprofessional muthafucka. I had been told Rashad to stop fucking with him he was too sloppy. After I heard that old bastard was looking for me, I made it known that I was looking for him. I was in Atlanta ready for whatever.

I pulled up to one of his stash houses and knocked out the biggest nigga in the house and told them to call their boss. I wasn't no punk and I was going to show him how I got down. I wasn't no hoe ass nigga and I could do dirt by myself. I didn't need an army of muthafucka but to watch my back I had my right-hand Pharaoh. Pharaoh was a tall lanky nigga with dreads. He reminded me of Snoop Dogg. He was a real rider though and ever since I had got out five years ago, he had been nothing but one hunned. He had the other niggas over there on the couch sweating through they balls. Since Pharaoh was a young cat, he was ready to bust them guns to prove to the streets that he was real. The nigga called Mr. Richards and Mr. Richards gave us an address. I let them little hoe ass niggas live. This wasn't my hood and if they ever thought about bringing, they little punk asses to Chicago then I would show them how a dirty south/Chi-town nigga got down. I had ran them Atlanta streets before since I was born and raised there. My daddy had once ruled over the whole city. Had Bruce weak ass not done that shit to Rebecca then my family would be in charge of the world. The shit didn't happen that way and we out here scraping like savages. I went to the address and was surprised that the address was a damn restaurant. At that moment I knew that nigga was scared.

He wasn't about shit. I thought that he would at least try to set me up since I had tried him, but he didn't even do that. He wanted to meet in a public place so that nothing could happen to him. He came to my car and explained that he did have my brother's wife, but she had gotten away. He was acting like he was trying to protect her, but I knew better. I knew that if she had not gotten away then she would have been killed. Now I was at square one trying to find her. Niya did not know how badly she was in trouble. I did not think that Mr. Richards would even go after her she did not know anything really. She was a runner for my brother, but it wasn't like she knew where he hid his shit or his money. All she knew was different locations to pick up product but hell that was a while ago. If Mr. Richards was smart, then he would have changed that shit every time he did a transaction. I guess when the FEDS picked her up, she told them that she would testify against Mr. Richards. She was too fucking stupid she agreed to that dumb ass shit. She was dumb I had told Rashad that the girl was not cut out for the lifestyle. I had only seen her a couple of times, but the girl was a nervous wreck every time I saw her. Don't get me wrong she was a gorgeous woman a little on the thick side, but she had the face to make up for that. She kept herself well maintained too and she had some damn good kids and that's rare these days. With these bitches these days they kids be smart mouth, dirty, and ratchet. I was happy that my baby brother had settled down for real. Rashad was always a damn player. I was never the type and when I met his sister Rebecca I fell in love. People always ask that shit like how could, I marry my stepsister since my Moms and Rashad's father had gotten married. Like I kept telling them I had never looked at Rebecca as a sister shit we used to fuck around when we were younger. When that shit happened to her I was so pissed and ready to murder any and every nigga that moved. It took baby girl so long to get out of that fucked up state of mind. Believe me when I tell you Rebecca is not the same person she once was and that is a damn shame. I married her because despite the mental breakdown I still loved her, and she was still loyal to me. No, we could never have kids of our own but who needed those problems. Hell, we had enough problems between trying to support ourselves and with the lifestyle we lived kids did not fit in it. Don't get me wrong I loved kids and I commended my brother for stepping up and taking care of Niya's kids. A nigga like me I did not have the time or the patience. That is why I was out looking for her and her kids. I wasn't going to let shit happen to them. I had got a text from a number saying that Mr. Richards had them. I tried to call back and no one ever picked up. I had tried calling Rashad and it said his number had been changed. I went by the house and it was empty. That is what has brought me to Atlanta but now I was stuck because I had no idea who sent me the text and how they knew that Mr. Richards had Aniya. I wanted to know why the fuck Mr. Richards wanted Niya so bad she really didn't know shit. Bing! Then it hit me, and I swore I saw a damn light bulb on top of my head. Niya was a runner for my brother and they went to different places to pick up the dope. That could only mean one thing and one thing only those were his main places that he stashed his dope. Yes! Jackpot! A nigga was about to come up on a fantastic lick! Niya's ass was going to have to wait because it was time for me to get this cash.

Chapter Twenty-Seven
CRENSHAW

I couldn't believe that I had betrayed my uncle he meant a lot to me, but he was foul. I loved him it had only been him and my Mom too. My mother was not liked by her family because her father was black. My grandmother had left Mexico when she was pregnant with my uncle Al. His father was abusing my grandmother, so she ran off to America to get a new start. She ended up in Texas there she met my Grandfather. From the stories I heard he sweet talked her, and they got married. Soon after that she became pregnant with my Mother. Things were going good for them until Wilbert who is my Grandfather started drinking then he too started beating on my Grandmother Marisol. She couldn't take it and ran back to Mexico, but she left Uncle Al and my mother Camille there with Wilbert. He took care of them for a couple of years. He did good too but one day coming home drunk he crashed his car and was killed instantly. Uncle Al and my mother grew up in foster care. My mother endured a lot of abuse from her foster parents, Uncle Al and her were placed together thankfully. Her big brother could not stop the boogeyman from sneaking in her bed at night. At twelve years old she became pregnant with Lucinda. She lied about who the father was to everyone. After she had my sister, they put her in foster care too. She became pregnant with me soon after. After she gave birth to me, she could not keep me as well she killed herself. When Uncle Al got older, he came looking for us. He found me first. I was adopted by Edward and Tracey. They were loving parents too who kept me laced with shit. Uncle Al found me when I was about five years old and he found me quickly because my case was open Edward wanted to make sure that I knew my biological family. We found Lucinda years later through an online search. I appreciated my Uncle because he never gave up hope. Over the years though he had changed from this loving Uncle to a nigga that I did not recognize. I grew up in Philadelphia and when I got older, I relocated to New

York. I knew after this I could not go home for a while. I had got caught up with this Niya chick and I didn't even know why. Niya was beautiful from her head to her feet I loved everything about her. I had a woman back at home Eshawna but she was nothing compared to the beauty I saw in Niya. When I found out how old she was I was surprised she was ten years older than me, but she was still fine and looked not a day over twenty. When I first met her, she was with that white boy Bruce he was a sucka muthafucka and I just knew that I was going to take her away from him. After that meeting, we had at the strip club I just knew I was going back home and strategize on how I was going to get that ass. I only went to the meeting because I was in town visiting my sister at the time and I was bored. Uncle Al had been my supplier for years and I just figured I would be nosey see what the old nigga was up to. When I called him and told him I was in town he told me to come to the meeting. After I went home my plan was to ask Uncle Al did, he know anything about her. When I got back home that hoe E had disappeared, she not only disappeared but she robbed my fucking safe at the crib. She was stupid I had been fucking with her for a year and I never trusted the hoe. She kept saying Crenshaw please trust in me and why you don't trust me? I gave the bitch a little bit of opportunity and she fucking stole the little chump change I had in the safe. It was funny to me because I knew the hoe was up to no good. She had been getting on my nerves talking that trust shit and I just wanted to shut her up and move on. I knew she was fucking with that nigga Rio in Brooklyn too, but I wasn't tripping he could have the silly hoe. I had given her the pass code telling her that if she needed anything that she should go ahead and get some money out of the there. You should have seen the way that hoe's eyes bucked. I knew that when I came back the money would be gone but I didn't expect her ass to tear up my house like she did. That stink bitch cut open my furniture, poured bleach all over my clothes, she did all types of shit to my crib. The joke was going to be on her though because although it looked like she had plenty dough on the outside it was hundred-dollar bill, then twenties, then fives, and ones and then it was all paper. Jokes on that stupid bitch all together she came up on six hundred dollars. She had lost a good nigga being stupid. I loved the girl too. She wasn't a looker but when I met, her she was one hunned all the way. She had a fat ass and no stomach. I had heard rumors about her still being in love with her ex. I couldn't believe it she had always been one hunned with me, so I asked her about it, and she told me that I was all she needed. I didn't really believe her but when six months came, and he got out of jail and nothing changed I allowed her to move in with me and we made it official. The whole time the bitch was trying to figure out my setup and how I ran shit so her and her man Rio could rob me. She had me fucked up. The cold part about it is that one of her friend's was the one who put the word out to me. And I knew it was real because Sheena and E was tight. Anytime E and I would get into I would have to damn near argue with Sheena too. It was like they were both my bitches. I hated that shit, but I secretly wanted to fuck Sheena. She was fine and she had a fat ass. Standing 5' 6 with an ass that could make traffic stop. She was caramel with long ass pretty hair. I think Sheena had a little Indian in her family. I wanted her bad too, but Sheena liked women damn shame. I used to think that her and E was fucking around cause she used to go too hard for her. One day I was chilling on the block with my niggas. My nigga Q yells out "Damn she finer than a muthafucka!" We all look and low and be hold it's Sheena. Sheena wasn't a known bitch neither she stayed to herself. She walked up to me and smiled "what up Crenshaw?" Her fine ass had my dick standing at attention that is what was up. "Nothing you looking for E? Now you know she

225

ain't out here." "Naw I was looking for you." I know she didn't mean it in a flirtatious way but that is how it sounded, and I was ready. "Shit alright." I put my arm around her neck, and we walked around the back. "Okay you can let me go." She moved my arm from around her. She was looking extra good in her army fatigue pants too. She had on a green shirt that only covered the top part of her body because her entire flat stomach was out, and she had a belly ring. "Man, what up Sheena? E done told you some fucked up shit about me again I am listening." She looked nervous. She blew out a breath. "Naw Shaw do not tell her that I told you this. Please do not tell her that I told you this okay?" She said and it looked like she was going to cry. "What up ma what's going on?" "I heard Rio and E talking about robbing you. They had been creeping for some time now. I thought that E was done with Rio but I guess not." She rolled her eyes. "Rio was my dude before he started messing with E and when I found out I cut both them off. When he went to jail E apologized and told me that she was just trying to show me that he wasn't shit. When he got out me and him got back up with each other. I had a feeling that they were creeping because E, had been acting funny. I started following them. I was sitting right behind their dumb asses at a movie they went to see.

That's when I heard them. I don't even know what movie it was, but I heard Rio yell out yeah that's how we gone rob that stupid muthafucka Crenshaw ain't that right baby he said to E and they kissed." I was fucked up behind the information I heard, and I know that Sheena was too. I could tell she wanted to cry so I pulled her in close to me and gave her a hug. She was a good girl and she did not deserve that shit. All this time E had me thinking that Sheena was a dyke. The girl had lied about everything. She gave me the location to where Rio laid his head and I put in the murder game after I got back to Atlanta. So E stupid ass was going to be looking stupid alone. She had tried contacting me, but I didn't answer because I didn't have shit to say. She was on the answering machine crying. Telling me how much she missed me, and that Rio had threatened her. She thought I was dumb because she was dumb no way I was falling for that shit. I looked over at Niya who was getting ready for work. She looked good but I could tell that she was mad because she had to start working again. Hell, this was going to be my first time working too. She had got a job at a laundry mat. We could not risk anybody finding her because she had changed her name. They paid her under the table, and they didn't ask for any identification. I on the other hand was working at

Walmart. I had to work but the good thing about me was that the police was not looking for me. Uncle Al was but he didn't know where I was and little did, he know that I was only an hour away from him. "Why you staring at me?" Niya asked looking at me while she put on her lip gloss. "No reason you look good as hell." I said giving her a kiss on her lips. "Damn Shaw you messed up my lips. What time you get off today?" "Nine tonight honey you gone have dinner ready?" "Of course, I am going to leave you a plate in the microwave." She said and kissed my cheek. "Alright be good sexy." "Naw nigga you be good I know how them bitches at Walmart is. Shit I worked there before straight thirsty." I laughed she always say that shit. I went to take a shit and lit my blunt. I was ready for the workday. I had never had a real job before all I knew was the streets. Being in this predicament made me have to get a job I did not know what I was doing. I knew one thing I knew the girl didn't have any money and I wanted to help her out. I liked Niya and I wanted to know where the hell was her damn husband? My uncle was looking for him and they got her. It was fucked up because Niya called him thinking everything was on the up and up. She didn't know how the game was played but shit her husband should have told her. Instead his punk ass just ups and leaves his wife to fend for himself. We needed to find his silly ass so that she could divorce him and marry me. I had to be honest with myself I did not want to leave that woman. She had turned me into a man. She asked me my life goals and I told her I wanted to own my own barbershop. I loved that she believed in me and I could see that is why Rashad kept her around. The nigga was a local joker and he was living in the hay day of his punk ass daddy. The shit was stupid if you asked me. Niya had told me all about their bright idea and I could not believe she went along with the stupid shit. Being with her had brought sense into my life. After two dirty bitches E and Talia a woman like Niya is a blessing. Niya was smart and she knew how to manage her money. Shit we were going to stack and then we were going to grab her kids and leave the country. That is what we needed a fresh start. I had family in Mexico and that meant that she had family as soon as she became my wife. I had told her this plan too and she just started kissing and hugging me. I loved this about my lady she was so affectionate I could tell that she longed for a man in her life. I asked her about her father, and she told me that when she found out about him, she would let me know. She told me about how her mother committed suicide and I felt her pain because my mother had gone out the same way. My mother was much younger though. Niya was an emotional mess because she found her mother in the bathroom dead. That had to be fucked up for her. She told me that they did not have a good relationship, but I could tell that it still hurt her. I finished my blunt and got ready for work. I jumped in my red pick-up truck. I had sold my Infinity to get the money so that Niya and I could have two cars. The way that we had our own work schedule somebody would have been left without a ride. I had a hundred thousand but Niya told me to keep it until we really needed it. We made enough money together and our rent wasn't shit. I paid all the bills with one check and I still had enough money to go buy shit. Niya would send money to her friend for her kids. I think the money was mostly to ease her mind about not being with them. She told me a little bit about her friend, and I knew one thing for sure she wasn't hurting for no paper.

Chapter Twenty-Eight
ANIYA

I could not believe that I had millions in the damn bank, and I could not even touch it because I was in hiding. That was some fucked up shit I needed the money because I wanted to get the hell out of this rinky dink ass town. I was living in the middle of nowhere working for pennies and nickels. I sent my checks that I did make to the kids. I had to figure something out I couldn't live like this forever. I was irritated the only thing good in my life right now was Crenshaw. He was wonderful. The first time we had sex was mind blowing. I had just gotten off my period and I needed the loving especially being around Crenshaw he was young and sexy. He had come back to the hotel after the trip back to Atlanta. He looked like he was stressed out and I felt guilty because I had put him in this predicament and turned his world upside down. He kicked off his shoes and headed to the shower. I had already showered and had on my black panty and bra set. Crenshaw had to purchase all my clothes and the only store we had seen was Walmart, but he hooked it up for me and I was still sexy in my Walmart merchandise. He got out of the shower twenty minutes later and he looked sexy all he had on was his boxers on. His long hair was in a ponytail. He sat on the bed and grabbed the lotion, but I snatched it away from him. He looked at me and smiled. I rubbed the lotion on his arms and shoulders I loved the way his biceps felt underneath my hand. He was so sexy, and he had tattoos all over this chest. I loved it. I gave him a little massage on his neck and shoulders. "That feels good ma" he said relaxing. I told him to lay down and he did, and I got up. I stood in front of him and dropped my robe to the floor. He smiled because he knew his patience had paid off. I had lost a lot weight from not eating the way I used to and my size 14 had come down to a size 10 but I still looked good. I did my sexy walk over to him and climbed in between his legs. I kissed his sexy lips and his breath smelled like peppermint and weed. I loved that shit. He had placed his arms around me and explored my curves. I kissed his chest and licked my way down to his belly. I took his dick out and it was big I knew that already. I smiled as I got up. I slid down on his pole and my box was in pain yet pleasure. I looked down at Crenshaw. "You better know how to ride this dick." He said giving my ass a smack. I laughed he just did not know I was a beast in the sheets. I never could understand why Rashad cheated on me because I did everything imaginable in bed. After a while of going back and forth I chalked it up as that was just him and he just wanted to be a whore. I left Crenshaw loving each and every, inch of me. I could tell the sex had him whipped because the look in eyes changed from me being a problem that he no longer wanted to deal with to this my bitch I gotta look out. I was the one who said that we needed to get jobs. Hell, Crenshaw did not have any priors, so it was not reason why he was out there hustling. I must admit I had forgot how it was having to depend on a check every two weeks. I knew Crenshaw had some money, but I did not want him to spend it. I wanted to save so when we moved, we could start our lives with the kids. I just hoped that he was on the same page as me. I really did owe him, and I was going to give him some money as soon as I could. I sat at the laundromat bored as hell. I hate when people came in and tried to talk to me. All they were trying to do was get in my business. Damn these country muthafuckas was nosey. They would just stare at me asking me who was my people? I would politely say "I don't tell people my business I am here to work not spark conversations" what the fuck was wrong with them. I could not believe this little town was so small and intimate. When Crenshaw and I moved in they were being so damn nosey then too. They tried every which way to try and get me to talk personally about myself. The truth was they couldn't handle my truth. Half the time I couldn't handle my truth. It was five o'clock and my shift was over. I didn't feel like cooking, so I went to Walmart and went to the deli. I saw Crenshaw in the aisle talking to some bitch that worked there. I was happy that I was looking cute I walked that sexy walk that I do right over to my man. Who the fuck was this young bitch? I thought to myself. She looked about twenty- one. She was cute enough, but she didn't have shit on me. He was talking about football and she was trying hard to flirt. Then I heard the words I had been waiting on. "So, do you have a girlfriend?" She asked twirling her nappy weave. The nerve of this little hoe to ask him but I wanted to hear his answer. "Yeah my lil mama Niy… I mean Amber." He said. I think he was getting the point that the girl was trying to flirt with him because he told her he had to get back to work and turned around and ran straight into me. "Niya I mean Amber what you doing here? You stalking me?" He asked smiling. The chick was still in ear shot and she looked over at me. I looked at her and smiled and then back to Crenshaw. "Naw bae I don't feel like cooking, so I came up here to get us some food from the deli. You always talking about their shit so good, so I want to try it." Sometimes he ate there on his lunch break. "I don't want none of that shit today baby. You can eat it just get me a Subway sandwich. I really wanted you to cook." He said looking disappointed. "Okay baby what you want?" I could not disappoint the man who had saved my life. "Naw you probably tired so I can just eat a sandwich." I noticed that the girl was still standing there listening. Damn where was management? I see that is why Crenshaw liked this job hell he didn't really have to do anything. When I worked at Walmart in Wisconsin they were on my ass. I grabbed his face and pulled it to me "what do you want to eat baby? I will make sure you get it." I gave him a peck. "You can't be doing that shit while I am at work." He looked around. "I'm sorry bae I just can't resist those sexy lips. But what you want to eat?" "I want a roast, some rice, and some lima beans. That shit sound good don't it?" I laughed "hell yeah okay I will hook it up." I was about to walk off when he grabbed my hand. "You need some money?" "Naw I got it." I said and walked away. I went and got my groceries and made sure to go back and check on Crenshaw in the electronic department. He was back there, and the same bitch was in his face. I had to walk up and say something because I was not having the shit. He saw me and smiled. The bitch probably thought he was smiling at her no bitch it's me again. "Damn I see y'all can just chill at this muthafucka" my statement made the chick turn towards me. "Hell naw people just lazy and don't wanna do work and be distracting you and shit," Crenshaw said. The chick didn't say anything she just walked away but I knew her pride was hurt. Thirsty ass hoe better back up off my man. I started laughing. "Shaw you so damn mean!" I said. "Man, on my life her breath stank, and she keep coming over here. She thinks she cute. Her damn hair look, like a bird's nest ugh. She trash ma I ain't fucking with her when I got you." He pulled me in for a hug. That is what the fuck I was talking about! This man that I had didn't have too much history with could see that I was worth more than just my pretty face. I had to jump through hoops and shit to get that kind of reaction from my husband. The man that I had given my life too and all he could do was fire a bitch. I knew that every time he fired them hoes, he was still sneaking too fuck with them. I was not no damn fool, and I knew that he was still pleasing them. If he wasn't then they would have caused his life a living hell because I know for a fact ain't nothing like a woman scorn. I went to pay for my stuff and headed home. I hated to go the house by myself because I felt so lonely. I put the roast in the oven in the shower. I loved the way the hot water felt against my skin and I sat there and cried. I did this about every day I let the shower wash my tears and sorrow away. I missed my children I had never been away from my kids for so long and this was harder than it looked. Crenshaw knew I was hurting, and I swear he made up for the loss of them. A mother could never just give up her kids and not think or worry about them. I washed my body and put on my gown and went to finish my food. I ate alone and watched television. I didn't even have anyone to call. Well I did but I didn't know what to say. Shit all I could think to say was I am okay. I did not know my next move or anything. Crenshaw and I was trying to figure that out. I still had not told him what happened with Rashad and he never brought Rashad up.

Chapter Twenty- Nine
CRENSHAW

I made it home and I could smell the food that had been cooked. I was starting to really love Niya and she didn't even know it. She made me smile when I saw her pretty face. I was happy that she had interrupted that ugly bitch Tasha that kept trying to push up on me. She stayed in my face and her breath really did stank. I had to check the bitch before I left work because she had the nerve to be disrespectful. She was talking to her little home girls. Juanita and another chick name Tasha. I walked past telling them bye. I don't know if the bitch thought that I couldn't hear her or if she thought she was being funny. "Girl his old ass girlfriend came up here. Girl she is old. Bitch damn near my Mama age." Her and the other girls started laughing. That bitch was lying. Niya did not even look her age the only reason the bitch knew that she was even older than me was because I told her when we were talking. Little bitch was just mad because I didn't give her ugly ass no play. Tasha wasn't a bad looking chick but everything else was bad on her so that made her ass ugly. She wished she was a thirty-six-year old woman that had two kids and still looked as good as Niya. All the young niggas that I worked with even was like damn that's your lady she fine. So, I know she was bad and I didn't need validation from nobody I knew what I had at home. I turned and walked towards her "what was that Tasha?" She started laughing "Aw Shaw you know that I was just playing but you know your girlfriend is old." She said laughing. The bitch thought I was a joke. "Tasha stop laughing cause your breath smell like shit!" I said and turned and walked off. She wasn't laughing no more and her "friends" had turned their laughter on her. I could just imagine all the shit that was going through her head. The audacity of her to even try to talk about somebody. My lady may have been a bit older, but her breath wasn't smelling like hot garbage. She was trash and it was seeping out of her mouth. I ate my plate and got in the shower. All types of things were going through my head. I was not cut out for the work shit, but we were trying to stay off the grid. My uncle had called and asked why I hadn't re up and I told him that I was going through shit with my girl. Which it was true, but he just didn't know my woman was Niya. He said he didn't care about her, but I know that if he ever figured I crossed him then he would try to kill me. Although that was no problem because I knew his organization I just didn't want to go to war with family. I got out the shower and looked at Niya sleeping. She was cute with her little red wig on. She had to buy a different wig every week because she slept in it. She didn't want me to see her hair underneath all fucked up. The girl was crazy she was beautiful to me regardless. I had never thought that I would find someone who I could settle down with, but I knew that I was falling for Niya even before this happened, we were friends. I knew something had gone wrong in her marriage. She still had not told me anything, but I knew that she would eventually I would have to wait around for it. I climbed in bed with her and wrapped my arms around her and kissed her neck. She backed her big booty up on my dick and although I wanted to fuck the shit out of her I was just too damn tired. This nine to five was kicking my ass. Niya and I never worked on Friday, so we decided to treat ourselves. We went to breakfast that morning. I loved spending time with my girl, and she looked so pretty. She had on a white sundress that went right below her knees. She was such a lady which was something I was not used to I always dealt with hood bitches and Niya was not one of them. I knew she was a rider though, but you can tell that she had been through some shit. We were sitting eating ice cream and she looked at me "So how would you feel if I told you I was pregnant?" I started laughing "I would say you fucking that white man that owns the laundromat." I had never told anybody, but I couldn't have kids. "Whatever why you say that how you wouldn't know that it was yours?" I looked at her and I told her "I can't have kids Niya. So, there is no way that you could get pregnant." She looked sad "damn Shaw I didn't know what happened? Why?" "Nothing ain't happen girl I just got a low sperm count. I been smoking weed since I was twelve shit so that could be the cause of it. I know my ex-girlfriend wanted to go see if it was her because she wanted to have a baby. We got the tests done and it was me." Talia knew damn well the doctors had told me that I couldn't have kids. A year later she ended up pregnant and I thought it was my baby. I was stupid for believing that it was a possibility. Niya still looked sad. "Damn though the thought of me not being able to have kids is scary. I love Deena and Malcolm so much I could not picture life without them two big head kids." I could tell she was going to cry. I knew she missed her kids and I wish I could take the pain away from her. I knew she cried every day she thought I didn't know but I could see the red in her eyes when she got out the shower. I grabbed her hand and I knew that nothing I said or did could comfort her. She wanted her children but the nigga she chose put her in a situation and got ghost on her. That shit did not make no sense that she had lost her children because he had started back in the streets. Shit didn't make sense to me because as far as I knew Niya had money good money at that. Shit they had companies and all types of shit and this fool wanted to be a drug dealer. I thought the idea was to get out the hood that nigga was a stupid muthafucka. I know one thing although the circumstances are shitty, I am glad that I got time to get to know her and I am glad that she got to know me.

Chapter Thirty
DARIEN

————⊶⊷⊷⊶⊷————

I pulled up at the first place that I and Pharaoh was going to hit. Man, when I put two and two together and figured out that he had been having Niya get from his main stash spots I called my bro and asked him for every location. This was sweet. Pharaoh was ready and I damn sure was too. Dressed and all black and my gun was the same color I cocked that muthafucka back and got out the all black Intrepid. I saw that the living room light was on and I proceeded to knock on the door. I already knew there was two niggas in there and I did not give a fuck if there was ten, I was getting this dope. I had Pharaoh knock on the door and the dumb ass nigga at the front asked who it was. We didn't say anything, and Pharaoh knocked again. You could hear him getting pissed and he yelled some shit in Spanish. He opened the door with an attitude and as soon as he did that, I pushed open the door. The other guy in there tried to bust his guns but Pharaoh was faster, and he popped his ass right in the neck. The other Spanish nigga was on the floor acting like he was so hurt. I kicked him in his ass "Get your bitch ass up and show me where the dope is." He got his bitch ass up and showed me where the dope was. Man, I thought we had hit the jackpot, but it wasn't really shit in there but two duffel bags. I looked in there and it was only four bricks and each bag what the fuck! Man, that wasn't shit I was looking for more! I needed more! It wasn't shit I grabbed the two bags shot that Spanish muthafucka in the head and rolled out. I had two more houses to hit and I wanted to do it tonight so that I could get back to finding that bitch! "Come on nigga let's roll out!" Two houses later Pharaoh and I was two million dollars richer. From what I could see I had two million dollars-worth of dope and I had a hundred grand in cash. The first house didn't have shit really, but the second house was where all his bricks was. Pharaoh and I had bust in that muthafucka guns blazing. I was pissed cause the first house didn't have shit and I felt like I was doing a blank mission but after I hit that muthafucking house it was on. We killed all five of them niggas. Fuck it I ain't have time to play. I kicked the door in. It was an abandoned house and at first, I was thinking ain't nobody in this muthafucka and that pissed me off even more. I kicked that muthafucka in and it was two Spanish niggas in there I shot my guns. BAM! BAM! I hit both they ass. A tall nigga came out the back with his guns, but Pharaoh caught him. I ran through the house and found the other punk ass niggas in the back trying to hide. Shit one of them was trying to jump out the window. I blasted they ass and right there in the back was where we found the dope. The last house it was just one muthafucka in there and I took his out quick. Pharoah scooped up the money and we were out that bitch. We went to the hotel and counted the money. Pharaoh lit the blunt and we smoked the rest of the night. I was excited shit I needed that money. After Niya had killed Bruce we didn't have any more money coming in from him. Rebecca was still running that little company but that wasn't shit. Those dudes that had raped her was still supporting us, but it wasn't enough. My baby Rebecca, I had her go out the country with my Mama and her Dad. Once we found out that Mr. Richards was getting arrested, we knew that he was coming for witnesses. I had my baby leave and I must admit that I missed her like crazy. I don't know why my brother just didn't have Niya go out of the country with them. After this I was going to go where they were too, I just needed to get my dough up and everybody know I ain't scared of shit. Mr. Richards is okay for now, shit didn't go through so the nigga is off the hook. Now that this was over, and I had come up a bit I was ready to go find Niya. I still had no idea where she was. I know Mr. Richards had told me that he thought that she was with his nephew Crenshaw, but Mr. Richards didn't know where they were. I don't know if she had told the nigga that she killed my brother, so I really did not want to reach out. The way it was looking I was going to have too. After the shit I did I was about to become a ghost. After two days of debating I went ahead and tried my luck and reached out to the nigga. I texted him to get a feel of where his head was? Mr. Richards had given me his number so it was time to take action and get her back so that we all could get ghost. 'What up this Crenshaw?' That's what I put. I waited for a couple of hours and I did not hear from him. Damn I wonder if it was his number. Pharaoh's girl had been blowing him up and I knew sooner or later I would have to take that nigga back home to his wifey. I had met Pharaoh when I was locked down and the nigga and I clicked. He was locked up on a bullshit domestic charge with his girl. He said the shit was so normal that he didn't even give a fuck. He said his girl and him would get into it over another bitch and they would be arguing. A neighbor would call the police and his ass would always get taken to jail. His girl never pressed charges so it would just be a violation of his parole for having contact with the police. He only served about five months that time. The nigga was a cool cat and he didn't fuck with too many just like me, so I took to him. I felt a vibration around ten o'clock that night. 'Who the fuck is this?' I texted him back in a hurry I didn't give a fuck about me looking desperate I was tired of looking for this bitch. Shit I was damn near about to give up, but I know my brother would not be happy about that. 'Darien I am Niya's husband bro' I waited for a response. Nothing, damn he needed to hurry up and answer so that this shit could be over. I heard a knock at the door. I knew it was Jessica. She was a bitch I had known when I was younger growing up in Atlanta, she was a stripper. I jumped up and answered the door it had took her long enough to get here. Jessica was a yellow bone with long black wavy weave. She was short as hell and she had the cutest face. Her body was bad as fuck. I loved the way her ass would shake while she walked. She came in and gave me a hug she smelled like weed. "What up baby girl what you smoking on?" She always had a blunt or something. "Damn Dee what up you missed a bitch or what?" "Hell, yeah I been thinking about your fine ass." I grabbed the bottle of Patron. "I got that gas for your ass nigga you know that nigga Trey keep me with that gas." She handed me the weed to roll up. Jessica had a man, but she had a soft spot for me. We had dated back in the day when we were younger. Jessica always been fine, and she has always been way too young for me. She was a good girl always though. I had dated her when Rebecca had been in the mental institution. Nobody knew about Jessica and I because she was too damn young for me. I was her first everything I broke her little virginity. We were trying to wait until she became a reasonable age to tell everybody. Shit happened though she got pregnant and her mother wanted to know who she had been fucking and she would never tell on me. Her mother sent her to Detroit to live with her father and he made her get an abortion. From what Jessica told me those Detroit streets ain't nothing nice. Her father ended up getting killed three years later and she was left to fend for herself. Her mother didn't want her to come back to Atlanta because she had moved on with her a new man. Jessica started fucking around with one of her Daddy's old ass friends and she started stripping. She didn't like his old ass when she got enough money, she bought her a ticket back to the A. She been here ever since then. She tried to seek me out but about that time I had gotten married to Rebecca. I felt bad about the shit. She met her man and he take good care of her. She loves the nigga but when D come into town, she made sure to treat me right. I mean no lie up until she met her nigga, I was helping her bills. I didn't just leave her out there because I did have a hand in fucking up her life. She was too young, and I should have just left her alone. It was something about that sweet pussy that I loved. I still had a soft spot for her little ass too. I rolled the blunt to perfection and sparked that bitch up. I watched as she twerked her ass for me. That's what we did when we met up. We would smoke, drink, and fuck. She turned the bottle of Patron and started drinking right out the bottle. She had on her pink panty and bra set and she looked sexy as hell. I loved the way she moved and although I loved my Rebecca I was still in love with Jessica. She danced her way over to the bed. She straddled my lap and grabbed the blunt out my mouth. She inhaled the smoke and grinded against me. I smiled at her she was so damn sexy. I put my finger in her pussy and she was wet just like she was supposed to be.

She threw her head back and kept grinding on me. I knew she liked it, but she didn't moan. That was Jessica for you when we had sex, she never moaned she would concentrate until she came. I picked her up so that I could place her on the bed. She was still puffing the blunt. I laid her on the bed and looked at her sexy ass smoke. I loved the way she puffed the blunt and I loved the way she was looking laying in my bed. That was one thing Rebecca didn't smoke and I wish she did because the shit was so sexy to me. She got up and her knees and moved towards me and handed me the blunt. She pulled down my basketball shorts and pulled out my 7 inches. She smiled and licked her lips. I was glad that I wasn't going home to Rebecca because the red lipstick that Jessica wore was going to stain. She put the entire dick in her mouth I inhaled the blunt. I watched as she went to work on that dick. She was bopping up and down and spitting on my shit. I thought damn. When we had first started out, she didn't even suck dick. I know that nigga had changed her, and it was for a good cause. Whenever I saw her, she gave the best head. I was about to come so I grabbed her hair and let her up. She stood in front of me and I gave her a shotgun the blunt was gone. I told her to lay down and she did. I grabbed her panties and pulled out my condom. I went straight and she tensed up. Her little pussy was good. She never said anything it was crazy. At, first I thought it was weird that she didn't say anything but over time I grew to like it. "D I'm about to cum! Yesss!" She said in her little sexy voice. I could tell she came because I could feel her pussy walls contracting. I kept going giving it to her. She had her legs to the ceiling, and I knew that I was wearing her out. I flipped her over quickly and started hitting it from the back and she was throwing it back. "Yes baby! I am cumming" she said again. She was throwing that ass back and I had to give it to her she knew what she was doing. I came and that was the end of that. Shit I didn't give a damn it was only ten minutes of sex shit she had cum twice. She kissed me and got up and got in the shower. I knew what that meant she was about to go back home to that nigga. I drank some more of the Patron because I knew she was going to take it with her because she loved to drink. She got out the shower and bounced. I was tired and I needed to get my rest because I had a long day ahead of me.

Chapter Thirty-One
CRENSHAW

I didn't know who the hell was this nigga talking about he was Niya's husband brother. I knew about Bruce, but he said his name was Darien. She had left early for work and I didn't want to bring it up because I kind of thought it was my uncle. I didn't know how the nigga had gotten my number, but I was about to find out I wasn't with the texting shit. The phone was ringing I thought he wasn't going to answer but he did right before I was about to hang up. "Hello" he sounded like he was sleep. "Yeah now who is this?" "Darien I am Niya's husband brother. Her husband Rashad." He cleared his throat. "Yeah what up?" I asked looking out the window. Nothing seems suspicious outside. "Shit what you mean what up? We looking for her shit. I know that she is in danger and from what I know your uncle is the one hunting her so what is you doing with her?" The nigga was cocky. "Man, I rescued her shit now where the fuck was you and your punk ass brother then?" "Fuck all that where y'all at?" He asked. "Nigga I gotta talk to her about this shit." This was crazy Rashad changed his number now he had his brother calling me something wasn't right. "What the fuck you gotta check with her for? Where the fuck is y'all at? She my damn brother's wife." This nigga was pissing me the fuck off. I hung up in his face I didn't have time for that nigga. This shit was getting crazy. I didn't know who the fuck Darien was. I had to find out more information.

Chapter Thirty-Two
DARIEN

———◦»»⦿⦿«‹◦———

That hoe ass nigga hung up on me. All I wanted to do was see where they were at? My brother wasn't even letting me know where the fuck he was at and he was only answering the phone sometimes. I had to find her for him, but I was close to leaving the bitch shit she seemed like she was alright. I got in the shower and decided to start my day. I could see that it was going to be a long one for me. I knew I had to get my nigga Pharaoh back to his wife and I knew that he was tired of the arguing. I knocked on his room door. He was awake and ready. I gave him half of the money and the dope and got him a rental. I shook his hand and headed back to the hotel. I didn't know what the fuck I was going to do because it didn't look like the nigga Crenshaw was going to give up the location. I was tired of sitting in one place waiting. It was just like being in jail. I hated it those three years that I was in there was fucked up. I was holding shit down but it ain't nothing like being out and being free. Just to sit there with a whole bunch of other niggas with no pussy and not being next to a sexy woman was enough to drive you up the wall. Then it was bullshit, every day with a hating ass nigga. So many niggas were on the down low but that was their business. I didn't get involved in that fag shit. I had me a little clique in that muthafucka that would fuck up anything moving. Italy the little broad that I knew from around the way came to stay with my brother. Rashad had let the broad live with him she was scandalous. The bitch was boosting, stripping, selling pussy, and selling dope for me she was a bad bitch. When Rashad told me about the shit that went on and how Italy was doing all that sneaky shit, I cut the bitch off. That night her brother was found dead in the shower. Shit she had fucked up and she knew her brother's life was in my hands. She had come to see me, and she was ranting and raving all types of shit. I had to come clean with Rebecca and tell her about the shit because I thought the bitch was going to snitch on me. Rebecca was pissed I thought she was going to leave me. She didn't know about none of the illegal shit I was doing. "Darien you so fucking stupid!" My wife yelled at me. "I know bae and I am going to stop doing all that shit." "No not that why the fuck didn't you think that I couldn't do the shit. I am your wife and I can be a ride or die too." She wasn't lying neither she was a real rider. Ever since she got out that mental institution Rebecca was never the same. The girl was so happy and innocent straight square but when she got out, she was evil. She was about them thangs and I wasn't even mad at her. She went through a traumatic event and it changed her. I loved her the same and because I loved her, I was not about to let her get in no type of illegal shit. I wanted her safe and out the way. You couldn't help but love Rebecca. Her green eyes were hypnotizing, and it was like staring into the world. You got lost in those eyes. Her body was always right, and she stayed getting liposuction if she even thought she was gaining fat. She was one in a million I loved everything about her. I had many women but there was only one Rebecca. I absolutely loved the fact that she could not have kids. I didn't want to be a family man I wanted to be a thug. I had to give many bitches abortion money to get rid of unwanted pregnancies This was even before that shit happened to Rebecca, I never wanted kids. I had this one stubborn bitch Mandy. Yeah it was about three of four years ago and I had to take not having a baby to a whole different extreme. I had been fucking with Mandy ever since I had got out jail for that little time I served. She was our neighbor that stayed down the street. Our mansion was huge and gated and when that fine ass white girl found out that I stayed in that house I knew she thought I had money. I had spotted her on the side of the road two blocks from the house. It looked like her Benz had caught a flat. She was fine with her tight blue jeans and red thigh high boots. I stopped and helped her. It was tough getting that tire on and it was cold as hell outside. That Chicago weather is nothing that I could get used to. I been living in Chicago for years, but I was southern born. She said she had called for them to help her, but they said that it would be three hours. Wasn't no sense in letting that beautiful lady sit in the cold. Her blonde hair was bleached, and she had brown haunting eyes. I loved the way she looked, and she had an ass that anybody would have to stop and stare at because for a white girl she had more ass than most black women. I knew she wanted the D right away I could tell. After I changed her tire, I told her that I would follow her home. Once she made it to her house, I let her know that I lived in the house down the street with the gated fence. Her eyes sparked up and I could see the dollar signs. Mandy was living with her parents and she wanted to marry into money. I told her that I was already married. Just like any other woman they developed some type of imaginary plan to make me want them and not want my wife. Mandy told me that she was on birth control but three months later and she was pregnant. We had only had sex three times. I was pissed when she told me she was pregnant. The weather was breaking a bit, but it was still windy outside. She invited me to come over. She stayed in the basement of her parent's house. She ran and kissed me. "I got great news big Daddy" she said smiling. Her little gray shorts were hugging her ass just right and I was enjoying the look of it. "Oh really" I said pulling her down to sit on my lap. "Yes! I am pregnant!" She said the shit like we were planning it. I looked at her like she had lost her mind. She knew I did not want kids that was why I asked the crazy bitch was she on birth control. "I thought you was on birth control" I said pushing her off my lap I was pissed but I was remaining calm. She looked confused as she sat on the floor "no I never said that." I rubbed my face she was pissing me off because she was acting stupid. This girl had set me up and I knew that she was going to be a problem. I grabbed a stack of money out of my pockets and threw it at her. "Get rid of it" I walked out. She had been calling me crying and shit, but I was not trying to hear it. I left her a text message to let her know that I was not leaving my wife and that she would be taking care of the baby by herself and I meant that shit. That was usually enough any smart woman would have taken that chance and got rid of it. No not this stupid bitch I didn't even hear from her but one day I was driving past with my Rebecca and low and behold who do I see Mandy. That bitch stomach was big and once I totaled up the months, I had to think she was about six months. I had to do something. I called her and she told me that she was keeping the baby. She still had my text messages and she was going to take me to court for child support when the baby was born. Wrong bitch! I dressed in all black went in her crib and beat the baby the fuck out of her. She was hospitalized and the baby was still born. I could not have that shit. Her family moved her away and I never seen from her again. I know that bitch knew it was me, but no police ever came knocking on my door. I loved Rebecca and although I would creep out on her I still loved her, and she knew it. I would kill anybody if I thought that they would jeopardize our relationship or call themselves trying to tell Rebecca anything about me. I knew her mental state was fragile and although I did dirt, I would never let that shit get back to the love of my life.

Chapter Thirty-Three
CRENSHAW

M y uncle had called a meeting with the entire squad. I was tired of this town, but I just didn't know where Niya and I were going to go. Uncle Al sounded shaken when he called. Although I had betrayed him in the name of lust, we were still family. I told Aniya I had to see what was up. I know it was fucked up to leave Niya behind, but I didn't know what else to do. To keep up my appearance I went and rented me a Challenger I didn't want my uncle to get suspicious. For all he knew I was trying to turn my life around. Atlanta isn't that far from where we are staying in Alabama, so the ride was short. I was a bit worried because of the talk that I had with Niya before I left. She was mad and I knew she was worried about me. "Baby girl we need to talk," I said as soon as she came home from work. I had got the call before I could even get out the house to head to my Walmart job. I called in and waited for her to get off. I could have easily gone up to her job and told her, but I did not want to scare her. She knew that I had betrayed my uncle, but I was hoping that he did not know. "What's wrong baby?" You could see the worry in her pretty brown eyes. "I have to go to Atlanta my uncle called a meeting." "What do you think he knows about us?" She asked looking afraid. "Naw I don't think so, but I just don't want to look suspicious." She started crying. "When are you leaving?" "Tomorrow I told him that I was close, but I didn't tell him where I was at." We made love that night and I decided to do something that I did not want to do. I texted that guy Darien back while I was on the road. I told him where Niya and I were staying. If my uncle was trying to set me up, then I wanted her to be safe. I asked her about Darien, and she told me that he was her husband's brother. That made me feel better I knew that he would keep her safe. I really had a soft spot for her, and I really wanted to make sure she was good. I kept trying to send the text, but I didn't have a signal. Damn stupid ass Boost Mobile phone. I kept on the way to my destination. I pulled up at my uncle's house and that made me feel better. There was only one car parked outside of my uncle's house. I went inside and saw my cousin Jeff with tears in his eyes. "What's wrong?" I asked. "It's Carlito he is gone they killed him" Jeff told me. Just then my Uncle came into the living where we were at. Carlito was my uncle's eldest son. He only had Jeff and Carlito. They were his pride and joy. "They killed my boy!" He yelled. His voice scared me a bit I had never seen my uncle so mad in his life. "What happened?" I was confused. "All three of my main houses got hit and they killed everyone! Everyone!" He yelled. "What you mean they killed everybody! What the fuck Unc what has been going on?" Worry was etched over my face. My Uncle looked at me with anger in his eyes. Then I saw the gun he was holding. "You tell me nephew because you seem like the muthafucka who I should be looking at." My eyes got big I know he was not saying that I stole from him. Yes, I did betray him by getting Niya away from him, but he had no business harming that girl. She had nothing to do with anything and she really did not know nothing. She had called him and told him that she was not going to tell. She trusted him and in return he was going to sell her and her child to the sex trade. He had to be kidding me. "What the fuck you mean?" I put my hands in the air in defense. I thought that Jeff was going to get up, but he didn't you could tell that he did not know what to think. "I mean the girl is gone then you disappear! Then my houses get hit! Tell me nephew what the fuck is going on?" Foam was damn near coming out of his mouth he was so angry. He didn't know shit and I was not going to give him any reason not to trust me. "I already told you that I had nothing to do with that girl getting away. I knew you thought I had something to do with that shit. I told you I needed sometime dammit I just killed two innocent children that shit fucked me up. I have murdered before, but I have never murdered kids that shit is traumatic. I do have a heart." I pointed to my chest. I was laying in on thick. My uncle knew I had no problem with killing anybody but for real I had never killed any kids before. I had told him that shit fucked with me because I had nieces and nephews around their age. I could tell he was buying it he put the gun down and broke down. "I don't know what to do. Carlito's gone and now I owe so much money!" I let him release his pain but inside I really did not give a fuck. He had made his own bed and to be honest he was about to kill me. "You don't know who did this?" I asked after a while. "No, no idea" Jeff said. That was my way to exit. "I am going to get out there and see what the fuck is going on," I said. I got up and headed on out. I was not coming back I did not give a damn what had happened. I did need to figure out a place for my sister and her kids though because once Uncle Al knew that I did not give a fuck and that I was not looking for who killed his son he was going to be pissed. I was done with that life. I loved my Uncle dearly but being around him you would be headed to nothing but destruction. I headed back to Alabama to get back in bed with my woman.

Chapter Thirty-Four
ANIYA

I was on pins and needles that morning when Crenshaw left. Ugh I hated this shit. He was going to make me kill him he was not answering his phone it kept going to voicemail. That stupid ass Boost Mobile phone he had I bet he didn't have no signal. I had decided to clean the house although it was clean, I still took my time out to clean it again. My mind was racing, and I didn't know what to do. I was scared to call Mya because I felt like the FEDS were watching her and I did not know if Tre would tell them I was here. I was just too damn scared. I needed to figure shit out. It was too much going on and now that I was alone everything was coming to me at once. I missed Deena and Malcolm so much that I did not know what to

269

do. I wanted to see them so bad, yet they were so many miles away. No place is too far to go, but I just did not want to get caught up and go to jail. I needed to do something all I kept doing was thinking about death and being in jail. I was tired of running I really was, and I really did want to see my kids. After much debate I think it was safe to say that it was time for me to go see my children. I needed to see them, and I wanted them to know that I was okay for now. I was going to wait for Crenshaw to get back if he came back and I was going to talk it over with him. I decided to make some food for us. I made some cubed steak, loaded potato, and broccoli and cheese. I cooked but I damn sure could not eat. It was past noon and I was watching a rerun of Love and Hip Hop Atl. I had missed it when it came on Monday. I loved me some Mi-Mi she was a bit timid, but she was a sweet lady. That Karlie Redd was something special with her messy ass. One thing was sure Stevie J could get it with his fine ass. I was sitting there laughing at Rasheeda for being stupid and naïve because Kirk wasn't shit when I heard the front door opening. I looked up to see the man I had been waiting for. My heart was so relieved. It was Crenshaw with his fine ass walking through the door. He looked like he was worried, but I ran and jumped up and hugged him. It was crazy how I loved this man so much. He was like Hakeem he had rescued me but at the same time he was my real knight in shining armor. After years of abuse, deceit, and being cheated on I knew that Crenshaw was sincere and the man for me. "Hey sexy you missed me?" "Hell yeah." I said kissing all over him "I am so happy you are okay." "Yeah Unc wasn't on shit he did suspect that I was with you, but I nipped that shit in the bud and spinned his ass. My cousin was killed and of his main dope spots were hit. He is in debt now with some Mexicans I think are his suppliers. He is about good as dead." He said. "Damn are you going to be okay?" I was worried was they targeting the whole family. "Yeah I will be alright. What smells so good?" He went to the kitchen. "I was nervous, so I got to cooking." I told the truth it had only been a couple of hours that he was gone. "Damn it looks good I am about to wash up fix me a plate babe." He went to the bathroom and I went to fix him a plate. I was so happy that my man was home. I made our plates my appetite had come back since I knew that he was okay. He came back and we ate. "Baby I want to go get my kids." He looked up from the table. "You think that would be smart?" He questioned drinking his red Kool-Aid. I shrugged my shoulders "I miss them" tears started falling. He got up and came over to me. "I know you do baby and shit if that is what you want to do then we will ride out. I want my sister to come with us too. Her and her kids I need them with me they the only family I have left." I smiled because this man right here was everything to me. I told him what I wanted, and he made it happen. I loved him so much I just could not explain it I knew this right here was real love. With Hakeem I was a broken woman who fell to him because he had rescued me. He took me from a fucked-up situation that I was in. I loved him for that and that is why I stayed. He controlled me and there was no way that I could have gotten away without his help, he made me depend on him. Bruce was someone who lied to me and promised me the world for his own personal gain. I loved Bruce because I thought he was someone different. He did make me into an independent woman, a business woman, but all that he helped me get and learn he tried to take it away. I loved him because he showed me how strong I was and how smart I really was. He saw the business savvy woman as a way to get where he wanted to be. Rashad was pure fucking lust. I jumped head-first into that marriage. No lie Rashad was a sweet man I give him that, but his mind frame was fucked up and ass backwards. He was almost forty years old and he thought that he was going to be a kingpin not in this day and age. What I hated most about Rashad was his disregard for me. He knew I loved him and all the shit I went through and he still put me through all that shit. What I loved about him was that he made me his wife. I know that he loved me. But the truth was Rashad was selfish and self-centered he only cared about himself and that is what made our relationship be in total ruins. Crenshaw and I were in the living room and he was smoking a blunt as usual. I was massaging his back when I heard something outside the house. "Bae you hear that?" I quizzed. My heart fluttered with panic. Crenshaw got up he looked out the window. It was about 7pm and there was still light outside. I got up and looked out the window and I damn shitted myself. It was Darien, Rashad's brother. That muthafucka was crazy. He must have known that I had killed Rashad he was coming for me. I had forgotten about him he had hunted me down and was ready to kill me. The way our house was set up he had parked on the street, but we could see him. He had to walk up a big hill to our steps. He couldn't see us looking but we could see him. "What the fuck that is Darien!" I said running to get my gun Crenshaw was right behind me. "Yeah that's your husband's brother I texted him to come help you when I went to Atlanta. He had been looking for you. I wanted to make sure you were safe, and he was the only person I could think to call." I looked at him in disbelief I took my pistol off safety "I killed my husband!" I said just then I heard the door being kicked in. I heard Darien footsteps we were quiet I held my breath and hoped like hell I shot quick enough. He turned to come up the hallway and when he got in the doorway BAM! BAM! I hit him twice and he went down his gun fell out of his hand. I was about to finish him off when he jumped up. I thought he was about to grab his gun, but he ran towards the door. I started shooting again but he was moving fast and zig zagging. He rolled down our big hill and once he got to his car, he jumped in. I didn't want to shoot outside so I let him leave. I turned around and behind me was Crenshaw with this gun raised at me. "What the fuck you mean you killed your husband?"

Chapter Thirty-Five
RASHAD

"I been hit!" That is all I heard as I started suiting up. I had to get to Darien. I wasn't too far either. I know he had on his vest, but he said that he thinks one of the bullets had went through. Damn! This was all my fault I should have went with him. He had told me the address of where I could find Niya. It was already bad enough that he had been looking for damn near two months. I could not believe that she had put herself in this predicament. I was on the highway going the speed limit. My thoughts were racing with so many questions. Niya was always doing shit first and thinking later. Why in the fuck would she tell Mr. Richards that she was not going to testify against him and her location? I thought she was smarter than that, but I guess I was wrong. Then she with some nigga Crenshaw she had lost her damn mind. That nigga was young too I just did not know what the hell was wrong with her. I should have just gone to see what the fuck was up with her and instead of sending Darien. The nigga had already threatened her. He says he did it so that she would want to stay with the police. What he did not know was that she had already did that stupid shit of telling Mr. Richards her location. He was so damn stupid that he didn't even have anyone to come and get her. Crenshaw and Jeff were his last options. She was so fucking stupid all she had to do was testify against Mr. Richards. She really didn't know shit. All she had to do was lie and they were going to relocate her and her kids. I don't know why the fuck she would tell him where she was at. Damn! This was too much. I know I had left her, and I ran off to go with my baby mama Talia, but I really did not think that the police would come and get Aniya. They wanted Mr. Richards in the worst way, and they did not give a fuck who testified. I thought that Aniya was going to testify and just get the heat off me but from what I knew she had called Mr. Richards. Darien had told me that he would bring her and the kids to me safely. No one knew I still talked to Talia they thought she disappeared on me. I was going to move Aniya close to me and explain everything, but things hadn't worked out that way. Aniya had fucked up everything. Talia didn't know I was married, and she didn't need to know. I was tired of her anyways and I really did miss Aniya and her the kids. I was mad that she had shot my brother, but Aniya was crazy like that. I pulled up at the house. It was shitty and it was on top of a fucking hill. Who the fuck lives on top of a hill? I got out of my new car I knew that I should have not been there but fuck it I had to see what she was on and where the fuck A'Deena and Malcolm where. Plus, she was with this nigga Crenshaw the entire time from what Darien told me shit he was Mr. Richard's nephew. I heard some arguing so I knocked on the door loudly. "Who is it?" Niya asked. "Me!" I said. I heard her walking to the door, and she was saying "who the fuck is me" her mouth had gotten real nasty. She swung the door open and she looked good. That gray wig was cute on her. I guess that was the new style silver hair. She had on some short purple shorts and I could see she lost weight she was fine as hell. She looked at me and her eyes were wide like she had seen a ghost well technically she had. "Rashad!" She screeched.

Chapter Thirty-Six
ANIYA

I just knew that I was not staring at my husband. I started stammering. "I shot you though." I said as he walked in. He was smiling from ear to ear like he was happy to see me. I was happy to see him, but I did not know what was going on. I needed to sit down. Crenshaw wasn't saying shit. "What up" Rashad said to Crenshaw. "Man, what the fuck is going on? She just told me she killed you." "Yeah she thought she did, but I am here as y'all both can see." He grabbed me and gave me a hug. He smelled good but where had he been? I pushed him away and went to grab me a drink. I poured me some of my Hennessey and looked at him. He was still so fine. "Look sit down so that I can explain everything." I downed my Hennessey and sat next to Crenshaw on the couch. I did not want to be next to my husband the person who I thought I had killed. Chapter Thirty-Seven Rashad "It was the third year that I had been working with Mr. Richards when the FEDS came to me and told me that they wanted me to help build a case against him. I wasn't with it at first and I told them straight up fuck them I wasn't no damn snitch. That's when they hit me with some real ass news. Cliff the guy who had taken the money from my Father was Mr. Richard's best friend." Crenshaw cut me off "yeah he died a couple of years ago." "Yeah he died but Mr. Richards and Cliff had used my father's money to come up. I talked it over with my father and he said fuck it gone head. I went ahead with the shit. That is when Niya asked me to stop making the runs I did not want her to be in direct danger. The phones were tapped and everything. So, I had been working with them the entire time. When Niya asked me to stop dealing with Mr. Richards I really did not stop but she never knew. I started fucking with females only because I needed to throw her off the other shit I was doing. I only let them give me head." I looked at her to make sure she knew that I never fucked them hoes. Well not all of them but I wasn't about to explain that to her. She shot me a look like I was full of shit. "Anyways somehow Mr. Richards found out that I was working with the FEDS that is when they told me to tell you. I was planning on telling you to that day but that is when you well you know." She jumped up "say it what did I catch you doing?" She was so damn crazy she was not going to let the shit go. "You caught Trickzy giving me head." I said. "Naw nigga and what the fuck did you say to me?" She looked from me to Crenshaw. She was getting on my damn nerves. "I said that I was going to be with both of y'all." I admitted. "I was just saying something though Niya you was acting a damn fool. I was trying to make you mad because I wanted to direct my mind to something besides the real shit. You know I love you girl" I reached my hand out to her. "If you love me then where the fuck have you been? Why the fuck was your brother trying to kill me?" "Niya I was mad at the time because you had caught me, so I just started talking shit. That day that you shot me I had on a vest and that is what you shot. There was no blood coming out of me I just fell, and I could not believe your ass stood over me and shot me again." I was not shocked at all by Aniya's actions. It was part of my plan. She was always talking about how she was going to kill me because I was cheating. I knew that she was about that life so that my plan to play dead. That day I was just talking shit to piss her off. I put the vest on and prayed that she went for my body and not my head. She did as I thought and shot me. When she left out the house I got in my car and headed to Jersey with Talia and my son. When Crenshaw called and told me that his Uncle had Aniya, I called Darien and told him that she was in danger. I never told him about my plan, I never told him about her shooting me I just told him to find her. I was a bit pissed that Aniya had shot him, but it was somewhat of my fault. I know she probably thought that he was after her and was trying to kill her. This was my fault and it was time for things to get back on track. "So why the fuck is you here now?" She burned a hole into my eyes with hers. "Girl I missed you, you are my wife." I shot the nigga Crenshaw a look to let him know that we were still married. "I wanted to know that you are okay. My brother was supposed to tell you to come with him to be with me. I know you were scared and that is why you shot him. I need you and the kids to come with me in witness protection. The FEDS don't know that I am here because I just left. Where are the kids?" Once she came with me, I was going to tell her that I was not in witness protection. Right now, I had to pretend because I didn't have any answers for her. She looked at me with irritation. She got up and went to the back. I knew she needed to cool down, but she would eventually calm down and come with me. I looked over at Crenshaw and he was looking crazy. Yeah young ass nigga she coming, back to where she belong I smiled.

Chapter Thirty-Eight
ANIYA

Rashad must have thought that I was a fucking fool. He had me and my damn kids running around here. I got kidnapped and shit, my kids was in fucking danger, and this muthafucka was too busy fucking hoes to let me know. Arrgh! He must think that I ain't shit, I went through too much shit and he gone come in here like he super save a bitch. Nah nigga where the fuck was you at when I was going through all this shit. I know he was somewhere living nice in fucking safety. I can admit that I was stupid for letting Mr. Richards know where I was, but I had no idea what was really going on. If my fucking husband had notified me or talked to me and let me know what his sorry ass was up to. It all could have been prevented. Then his dog ass got the nerve to say he never fucked none of them hoes. He a muthafucking lie! Crenshaw came to check on me. "Niya you alright?" I shook my head no and he came and hugged me. We had the door closed so that Rashad couldn't see us. It felt so good to be in Crenshaw's arms. He was so sweet he was a real man he smelled good like his Usher cologne. I needed him in my life I closed my eyes I remember the day that I had to kill Hakeem. Tears streamed my face as I thought back to the good fight we had. All those beatings I took. I thought about the relieved feeling I felt once I didn't hear him any longer. I thought about the day that I knew I was going to have to kill Bruce. He was trying to take my livelihood. I thought about Rashad and how I felt betrayed. These niggas had turned me into a cold-blooded killer. I remember the days that I was held captive by Mr. Richards, and I was so scared. This nigga could have helped me, but he didn't. I was having those dreams that were tripping me out at first, I thought they meant something, but I know that I was close to death and I was hallucinating. I have been close to death and my children could have been killed if Crenshaw had not been the man that he is. I stopped hugging Crenshaw. I dried my eyes. "You alright?" He looked at me. "I am all good baby I will be in there in a minute I gotta get myself together." Crenshaw left out the room and closed the door. I grabbed my gun off the dresser and said a prayer. "Lord please forgive me for I have sinned. I have been through so much. No that does not give me the right to go around ending these men lives, but I feel that my back is up against the wall. I have no other option. Thank you for protecting my kids and I. Please forgive me for what I am about to do I am sorry well, not sorry but I know that it is a sin and I repent in the name of Jesus. Amen." I opened the door to the room and walked out. Rashad was still sitting there looking like the scum of the fucking earth. I do not even know why I loved him. Yes, he was fine as hell and could lay pipe but so could Hakeem, and so could Bruce. I smiled at Crenshaw his young fine ass. He had risked it all, he had lost everything. He loved me and this time I was not the one risking it all he was and that spoke volumes. I raised my gun and fired at Rashad he didn't know what hit him. I made sure to aim for the head this time. Crenshaw jumped up "what the fuck Niya!" "Calm down fuck him. He let me and my kids be in danger then gone sit his ass up here like he doing me a favor. I could have lost my kids. Are you going to help me bury him in the backyard or what?" I said. Crenshaw started laughing. "You was tired of that nigga huh babe?" We buried Rashad in the backyard of that house on the top of the hill. We left his car in Atlanta and went to go get Crenshaw's sister and kids. I was going to Wisconsin to get my babies. These niggas had turned me into a killer, and I was hoping like fuck that I was not going to have to kill Crenshaw. He seemed like he was on the up and up but so did Hakeem, Bruce, and Rashad. Those niggas had turned me into the woman that I am today, and I thanked them for it. I may not be perfect but best believe I ain't taking no shit.

The End!!!!!!!

ABOUT THE AUTHOR

New York Times & International Best Selling Author Billie Dureyea Shell was born in Compton California and now lives in Ladera Heights with his wife and kids who he loves to spend time with.

He is the Owner of several properties in the Los Angeles area and gives back to his community by providing low income housing to those who need it.

He stated "It doesn't matter where you at or where you from it's what you do with your time. There's nothing you can't do if you put your mind to it".